True Story Of the Perfect 36

By Veronica R. Tabares

Paperback Edition

Cover art by Bridgitt Tabares

Sun Break Publishing, Seattle, WA

Published by Sun Break Publishing, 4616 25th Ave NE
#372
Seattle, WA 98105.

Library of Congress Control Number: 2019917122

ISBN: 978-1-60916-021-0

Publishers note:
The Perfect 36 is part of history, but that doesn't stop
this book from being a work of fiction and a figment of
the author's imagination. With the exception of public
figures and historical events, any similarities to actual
characters, places, names, or events are purely
coincidental.

To my sister, Dena, who insisted this story needed to be told.

You know what, Sis? You were right!

PROLOGUE

All is quiet in a lonely countryside as a train chugs merrily along its predetermined path.

Peaceful. Serene.

The countryside's beauty is undisturbed by the train. As a matter of fact, its prettiness is enhanced by the train's hardworking smokestack, which decorates the horizon with billowy clouds, much as a child uses her favorite crayon to decorate her most recent masterpiece.

Idyllic. Placid.

All this calm and peace is shattered as the train's whistle blows unexpectedly, startling a nearby flock of birds into flight. As the flutter and flap of wings and the piercing screech of the whistle fades away, a voice takes its place. The voice belongs to a woman. Calm and assured.

"People think they know history," the voice

states bluntly.

The voice belongs to Vanessa Rossi, a time-traveling mother with the weight of the world on her shoulders. And although this story is not about her, she does have an important part to play.

"Facts set in stone." Vanessa's voice strikes like the hammer to the anvil. "Old. Boring. Solid. Dusty."

Vanessa is pursuing a degree in archaeology and knows all about dusty old facts. There are a number of them she has dug up herself.

"Unchangeable," she states firmly, as if it's the end of her statement.

The train in the distance takes an unexpected curve around a mountain. As the tail end of the train disappears from sight, the omnipresent voice of Vanessa continues, this time more softly.

"But history doesn't record everything. It can't. Not when it's mere mortals, fallible women and men who do the recording."

Suddenly, out of nowhere, the train reappears and zips by a logging town that seems to be stuck somewhere in the late 1800s. The town is disturbingly ghostly in appearance. There are no people visible, just buildings. But the train, like time, doesn't care about minor details such as the absence or presence of people. It powers past the town and plows into a forest.

"Take for example the day Tennessee ratified the Nineteenth Amendment and American women, after seventy-five long years of struggle, got the right to vote."

The train clears the forest and suddenly, out of nowhere, a bridge appears. Undaunted, the train follows its track and chugs across it.

"Boring you, am I? Think you already know this little piece of history?"

A mountain rises straight ahead, in the direct path of the train. From overhead it is obvious that the builders of the tracks miscalculated. They did not wrap the tracks around the mountain as before. The train heads toward a disaster of monumental proportions.

But the train chugs on, unaware of its doom. It picks up speed on a straight patch of track, while the mountain does what a mountain does. It remains an impassable obstacle.

Doom speeds ever closer. The train is now going so fast it could not possibly stop in time to avoid the upcoming crash.

The train clears the last few trees before the mountain when, miracle of miracles, a tunnel appears. The train, unperturbed by its brush with disaster, whisks into the tunnel. Nearby leaves and twigs dance merrily in its wake.

"Well, you've never heard this story." Vanessa's voice is a welcome distraction from the recent tension. "The *true* story. It's not written down in any history book, anywhere."

On the other side of the mountain the train explodes out of the tunnel into the bright light of day, its whistle blowing shrilly.

Chapter 1

"WANNA PLAY A GAME?"

Zoe's sweet voice broke through the wall of worry that surrounded Vanessa, that always surrounded Vanessa.

Vanessa, a petite blonde decked out in jeans and a purple University of Washington sweatshirt—typical daily wear for students at the university—always had a lIst of to-dos a million miles long. As soon as she completed one chore, five more popped up in their place.

She set a bag of groceries on the kitchen counter and pushed away the thought that pursuing a college degree *must* be easier for people who didn't have children.

Not that she regretted the degree or the children, but she couldn't help having the occasional outlandish daydream in which she sat alone in a quiet room studying, for a full hour, without being interrupted. No squeaky little voices that constantly demanded her time and attention. She could get ahead in her studies instead of scrambling to complete each assignment minutes before it was due.

Who was she trying to kid? She loved those little voices, along with the children they belonged to. She turned to her daughter and smiled.

"What kind of game, sweetie?"

Years of practice had taught Vanessa how to keep her voice gentle and hide the stress that lurked just behind her eyes. She knew she had no time to play games. She had work to do. Lots and lots of work.

But she also knew that in a child's eyes, *play* was work, and one of the most important things in the world.

So, after dinner, and after she'd supervised her children's homework, there was that paper due tomorrow she still had to write, and a textbook to read, and several—

As Vanessa spiraled down a whirlpool of worry her eyes darted around the room frantically, until one fortunate dart brought them to her little daughter's hopeful face. Faster than she could snap her fingers the entire list of to-dos melted away, along with a tidal wave of stress.

All those stressors—dinner, homework,

chores, bills—were just that, stressors. They could wait. She'd allow them to take over her world again after playtime.

Because children stayed children only so long. Every day they grew up a bit more, became a little more independent, took another step toward adulthood.

Which made playtime an ever-dwindling commodity, and therefore precious.

Especially since at eight, Zoe was still in that prime bonding stage. Memories of a great family life and a fun childhood could be built daily.

Vanessa smiled at her little daughter as these thoughts zipped through her brain and came full circle back to the present moment. Playtime. Yes. Playtime was just what she needed.

It wasn't just that classes had been challenging lately, although those had been difficult enough. But Tony was due to go out on another two-week-long flight the next day, the second in three months, and lately her oldest daughter had shown signs of becoming a teenager. Based on her attitude, she already was one.

As Vanessa reached out to put a hand atop Zoe's wispy light brown curls, she noticed that

Zoe's sweater was drooping off one shoulder, again. For some reason no one in the family could figure out why Zoe preferred to wear her sweater ragdoll style rather than like a normal person.

Vanessa did what she always did. She gently pulled the sweater back where it should be. Then she bent down until she was eye-to-eye with her hopeful daughter.

"You get your sisters, I'll get your dad, and I'll meet you outside. Think about what game you'd like to play. Okay?"

Zoe nodded and smiled happily. Vanessa noticed, but ignored when the sweater slipped from Zoe's left shoulder again. That would be a battle for another day.

"Let me just put the frozen stuff up first," she said as she reached into the grocery bag and pulled out a couple of bags of frozen vegetables.

"Mom?"

"Yes, sweetie?"

"Tag, you're it!" Zoe's hand flashed out and touched the surprised Vanessa on the arm before Vanessa could realize what had happened. Then in a flash the munchkin was out the door and out of reach.

"That sneaky little monkey." Vanessa

chuckled. She shoved a bag of frozen peas in the freezer behind the chicken and slammed the freezer shut. "Guess I'd better go tag Tony. That'll get the game going!"

And it did. In less time than should be humanly possible, the entire Rossi family was cavorting around the front yard enjoying a rousing game of tag. Even twelve-year-old Becca, with her perfect hair and nails, had been pulled outside to run around the front yard with reckless abandon.

Not that she had allowed herself to stoop to anything so awkward as running. She was entirely too conscious that if even one of her friends walked by and witnessed her participation in such rowdy behavior it would ruin her reputation as a cool girl. And being a cool girl was everything!

Besides, she had spent thirty minutes straightening her long brown hair until it lay like silk down her back. There was no way she was going to chance—

"Tag!"

Eleven-year-old Maddie mussed some of that silky hair as she slapped Becca on the shoulder. Normally Becca would have been furious, but Maddie got a pass. Most likely since Maddie had hair nearly identical to

Becca's and knew what a hassle it could be to take care of it.

"Tag!" Maddie repeated, this time so loud even a statue would feel the need to respond.

Becca gave her a dirty look that would have cowed anyone but a sister.

"Get Dad! If he catches you when he's it, he'll toss you in the air. It's fun!"

Becca's eyes lit up at the memory of past games when she had been tossed in the air with wild abandon. Or at least that's how it had seemed to her. The feel of the floating freely—

"Becca," Maddie hissed in her ear and gave her a little go-on-get-moving push. "You're it!"

Becca would've joined in the game, which looked like fun, except she saw movement out of the corner of her eye and feared one of her friends might be coming down the street. So, instead, she used her big sister voice to call over the four-year-old munchkin, Audrey, and gave her a big hug.

"You know what, Audrey?"

"What?"

Becca brushed a lock of blonde hair from her little sister's forehead and kissed it lightly. Then she stepped back and smiled.

"Tag," she grinned at her youngest sister, "you're it!"

Some four-year-old munchkins might be upset by such trickery. Not Audrey. She giggled and made a beeline across the yard to her father.

"I'm it, Daddy! I'm it!" she yelled gleefully.

Tony, looking athletic in his jeans and black University of Washington sweatshirt, did what any good dad would do. He pretended fear as he ran away from his little one just fast enough that she couldn't catch him right away.

So, when she did get close enough to grab his sweatshirt and tug as she yelled, "Tag!" it was a satisfying experience. And the satisfaction was boosted to the moon when Tony grabbed his daughter and tossed her high in the air. Her squeals of delight during those glorious seconds of untethered flight told the whole story.

Tony caught Audrey and gently set her on the ground. She instantly ran over to her mother to give her an ecstatic hug.

"Me next! Catch me, Daddy!" Zoe yelled.

So, he did. And after Zoe got her glorious seconds of flight, she wrapped her arms around her father's neck and squeezed tight.

"I love you, Daddy, so much!" she said happily.

"I love you, too, Zoe-girl," Tony told his

daughter as he returned her hug.

Vanessa smiled as she watched this father-daughter bonding moment. It did her heart good when she saw her daughters—

As soon as the word *daughters* popped into her head she automatically looked around for her youngest one and was horrified to discover that the munchkin was nowhere in sight.

"Audrey!" she yelled in a panic.

But before her heart had the chance to skip even a single beat Becca and Maddie marched into sight from the side of the house, Audrey between them. The fact that each girl had a tight grip on one of Audrey's hands told the story that the little one had not come willingly.

"We've got her, Mom." Becca grimaced at her youngest sister.

"She was on that lattice thing," Maddie added, mirroring the displeased expression on the older girl's face.

Not that Audrey cared one wit for displeased expressions, even if they were on the faces of her beloved older sisters. She had a plan and needed to see that plan through.

She had just wiggled her hand free from Becca and turned to work on Maddie's side when she felt a hand on her shoulder. Audrey looked up to find that her mother had knelt down to her level and was looking at her with concerned eyes.

"Audrey." Vanessa wrangled together all the patience she could muster to keep her voice calm. "What were you doing?"

"I want to ply like a pairy." Audrey's reply was calm and serene, as if jumping off the roof was an everyday occurrence and nothing to worry about.

Audrey may have only been four, but even a four-year-old knows when she's upset her mother. So, when Vanessa's eyes flew to the roof and her face blanched whiter than mashed potatoes, Audrey was quick to reassure her.

"I won't pall, Mama." Audrey placed her free hand on her mother's arm. "Daddy's here."

But Vanessa was not reassured. She shot another glance at the roof and gulped at the thought of Audrey flinging herself from that height. Then she took a firm hold of Audrey's arm, just to make sure the child remained safe on the ground, and closed her eyes, as if in pain.

Becca shot a quick look at the roof and grimaced at Maddie. Maddie returned that grimace and added an eye widening in response.

This was not the first time their little sister

had had to be rescued from a dangerous situation. Audrey had been given the nickname Stunt Baby at the age of eight months when she skipped crawling entirely and went straight to running and climbing. Her physical prowess far outpaced her mental ability to recognize danger. She had no fear.

That made Vanessa's job as a mother agonizingly difficult.

Vanessa sighed and opened her eyes to look at her little girl. Raising this one to adulthood was going to be quite a struggle.

"We're done with tag," she declared. "Time for a snack, then homework."

"I don't have homework," Audrey said.

Before Vanessa could decide what to say, Tony grabbed Audrey and swung her onto his shoulders. The little monkey giggled happily. There was nothing she liked more than being up high.

"Hey, Dad." Becca stepped closer to her father and tickled a bare spot on the top of her sister's foot. Audrey wiggled happily. "Know anything about the Nineteenth Amendment?"

"Paper?" Tony asked as she grabbed Audrey's leg with one hand to keep her from squirming off.

"Presentation." Becca grimaced. "Poster,

speech...the whole works!"

Tony thought for a second before he snapped the fingers of his free hand. With the other hand he kept a tight grip on his youngest daughter since she might at any moment decide to jump down or climb higher.

"Ever hear of the Perfect 36?" he asked.

Becca shook her head.

"You'll love it." Tony smiled at the thought of sharing this piece of history with his daughter. "Women getting the right to vote came down to a single letter."

"A letter?" That sounded interesting to Becca. "Which letter?"

"Not that kind." Tony smiled as he shook his head. "The kind you mail."

Tony scooped Audrey off his shoulders and set her on the ground. She immediately teared up. She liked being on her father's shoulders.

"C'mon buttercup, suck it up," he said as he lightly tapped his youngest daughter on the nose.

"What does that mean, Daddy?" Audrey asked with a sniff and a smile.

But before Tony could answer, Vanessa grabbed Audrey's hand in a firm grip and led her to the front porch.

"Mommy, what does that mean?" Audrey

asked as she allowed herself to be led inside.

"Daddy's being Air Force-y, sweetie." Vanessa threw a smile Tony's way before she turned back to her daughter. "Snack time!"

The magic words *snack time* were all it took to not only get cooperation from Audrey, but Zoe as well. With nary a word Zoe skipped her way into the house with her mother and little sister.

"Anyway, it's a great story," Tony said as he turned to Becca to continue their conversation, almost as if there hadn't been an interruption. "Learned about it in one of my classes. I think..." He paused for a moment, then smiled. "Yes, I'm pretty sure I still have the book!"

The good father led his two daughters into the house in search of the right book.

Chapter 2

IT WAS OFFICIAL. PHILIP was not only out of place, but out of time.

Well, the place was right. His destination had been Portland, Oregon. There were signs all around with *Portland this*, and *Oregon that*. The place was right.

But he'd been aiming for the turn of the century from 2900 to 3000.

This was not it. He had misjudged. Quite possibly by an entire millennium.

To make matters worse, he stuck out like a sunflower in a field of lavender.

It wasn't just his clothing that made him stand out, although his shiny, flowing tunic with its matching pants and jacket—fashionable in the year 3027 but not so much in this time period—certainly did that. It was more. His Adonis-like good looks. His ramrod-straight posture. His ultra-smooth skin.

Not to mention that he couldn't help looking like a tourist. That was the real giveaway that he didn't belong.

Well, if he looked like a tourist, he might as well be a tourist. He doubted he'd get another chance to visit this place and time. He'd might as well look around a bit. No harm in simply looking.

As Philip strolled through the downtown area his attention was drawn to a window through which he could see movement inside. Curious, he moved closer to check it out.

The window spread across nearly the entire width of the building and was decorated with words and drawings of people sitting at tables together. Fancy letters across the top proclaimed the promise of a HAPPY HOUR with friends and food.

Philip had read of this practice in some of the older history books. Restaurants and bars from this ancient time period would lower the prices of their wares at certain times of day to bring in more customers.

Philip stood in front of the window for several minutes and watched the faces of those inside. It did indeed look like they were having a happy hour.

He knew he should stay outside. Walking

around the town was one thing, but he absolutely must avoid close contact with these people. He—

The door opened and three women exited, laughing together as if they had not a care in the world. Philip quickly slid inside. He couldn't help himself. As a scientist, the temptation to witness, firsthand, cultures of the past interacting, going about their daily lives... It was too good of an opportunity to miss.

But as he stepped over the threshold, Philip paused. What he was doing was dangerous, and he knew it. Any interaction with these people of the past could, potentially, cause a ripple in time that would be felt even in his own distant time.

A woman in the back of the room cackled merrily, causing Philip to look in her direction. These people were so relaxed, so...so...happy!

The lure of the laughing voices got the better of Philip's common sense and he decided he'd chance it. Surely there'd be no harm if he spent a few minutes absorbing the atmosphere.

Without further thought he casually walked to the bar—as casually as a man more than a thousand years out of his time could—and sat on an extremely uncomfortable high stool. He wiggled a bit to activate the cushions of the seat, but the stool continued to feel like the hard, cold steel it was.

"Hmm," Philip muttered, "must be broken."

Chapter 3

DOUGLAS WHITFIELD WAS DISAPPOINTED. Every day for the past month he had spent hours in this restaurant buying drinks, shaking hands, and chatting up every man in the place. All in the hope that he'd find a contact or connection that would help him with his new project.

The net result had been a hole in his budget the size of Wisconsin and a deep desire to avoid happy hours for the rest of his life. Longer, if possible. He had found no deep pockets and no connections. Zilch. Zippo.

So much for the rumor that this restaurant was the favorite haunt of Portland's most innovative movers and shakers. Every guy he had met here were wannabes. Wannabe CEOs, wannabe inventors, wannabe chefs...and even a few wannabe actors.

Douglas was in his forties. He didn't have

time to wait for a "wannabe" to become an "is." He needed to befriend and get in tight with a success rocket who knew how to make things happen, and he needed to do it yesterday!

A flash of light caught Douglas's eye and he watched as a tall, handsome man dressed like a glittery guru stepped through the doorway, unsure of himself.

"Actor," Douglas muttered under his breath as he turned away in disgust. "No use to me."

But when the man in the tunic sat next to him at the bar, Douglas gave him a second look. He wondered if he'd misjudged the guy. There was something unique about him, different. He certainly didn't act like any actor Douglas had ever seen, and the fabric of that tunic...

Douglas made a split-second decision that this man might be worth cultivating. He had that smooth, polished look that only the very wealthy could manage.

Next best thing to a mover and shaker was a man with more money than he knew how to spend. And any man who dressed like an alien guru must have more money than was good for him.

Douglas swiveled around to the newcomer and studied him closely, trying to decide how best to start a conversation. When the man patted his pockets, as if looking for his wallet, Douglas made a sign to the bartender to bring food and drink for two.

∞

Philip was fascinated and wanted to absorb every ounce of energy, every nuance of culture, in the room. There was nothing, nothing, like this where—or more precisely when—he was from.

He grinned as he read writing on the wall and realized it was a menu. How quaint!

It would complete his experience if he could taste a sample of this antiquated style of cooking. He was pretty sure they still used gas and electricity as fuel sources during this era. It would make a difference in the taste of the food.

He patted his pockets, trying to remember where he'd stashed the currency for his trip. Then he remembered that this particular time period was not his destination. He had no appropriate currency. He would not be able to participate.

No food for him!

Philip's shoulders slumped as he realized just how much of a failure this trip had become.

He had missed the time mark by nearly a thousand years. And now the opportunity to taste—

"Hello, friend!"

He jumped as a voice interrupted his thoughts. The voice belonged to a man sitting at the bar beside him. The man who had his hand extended, as if he wanted something.

Philip blinked several times as his brain scrambled to remember what he could about the customs of this time period. There was something about an outstretched hand gesture. If only he could recall what it meant, and how he was supposed to respond.

Finally, it hit him. People still clasped hands and waved them about as a sign of friendship.

Although why it was a sign of friendship Philip had never understood. But he needed to blend in, so he awkwardly took Douglas's hand in his and began to wave. He was so caught up in the process of the handshake that he failed to notice the odd look Douglas gave him, or how quickly he pulled his hand away.

"Name's Douglas Whitfield," Douglas said. "Where ya from? 'Cause…"

Douglas motioned to Philip's outfit. Philip looked at Douglas's clothing, then at his own, and realized for the first time just how out-of-place he must look to these people. As one of the premier time travel theorists it was embarrassing how many mistakes he had made.

"Umm…"

"Never mind. Not my business."

Douglas studied Philip for several awkward seconds, then nodded as he obviously came to a decision.

"Bet you could use a friend." Douglas slapped a fist on the bar. "And a drink. I'm buying."

The bartender arrived with two plates of food and two beers. Philip's eyes widened as the bartender set one plate in front of Douglas, and the other directly under his nose.

"What d'ya say, friend? Care for a bite?"

Philip's stomach gave a long, low growl. Douglas grinned knowingly.

"I'll take that as a yes. Dig in!"

As if to illustrate what he meant, Douglas picked up a slice of pizza from his plate and took a big bite. Philip, not knowing what else to do, copied him.

The pizza was hot, fragrant, gooey, and absolutely delicious. Philip closed his eyes as he enjoyed the experience of his first bite of pizza. Heaven!

When he opened his eyes again, he noticed that Douglas had a mug in his hand and was drinking a foamy, yellow liquid. He grabbed his own mug and took a swig.

He hadn't known what to expect, but it certainly wasn't this. The bitter brew assaulted his taste buds and made him regret the large mouthful he had sucked in. Not knowing what else to do he swallowed the beer.

"What is this?" he asked, unable hide the disgust in his voice.

"It's a local brew," Douglas explained. "A bit on the bitter side, I agree. But you'll find it pairs well with the food. Take another bite of pizza."

Philip gladly took another bite and was surprised to find that its flavor was, indeed, enhanced.

"Now another drink of beer," Douglas prompted.

Reluctantly, Philip raised his glass and took a sip. The sip turned into a swig and a smile blossomed on his face.

"See, not so bitter this time, is it?"

"Not at all," Philip replied as he took another swig.

"Enjoy, my friend." Douglas slapped Philip on the back. He looked around and noticed a vacant table. "Let's move over here. Where it's more comfortable."

The two men moved their food and drink to a nearby table and sat. Philip looked at the plate of food and mug of beer like he was unsure of the next steps.

"Eat, drink, and be merry!" Douglas laughed at the man's hesitation. "It's not going to bite you!"

Philip looked at the happy faces around him. The restaurant was indeed filled with people eating, drinking, and being merry.

It was a fluke that he was in this time period in the first place. He might as well take advantage of his visit and enjoy himself. He picked up a new slice of pizza and shoved nearly half of it into his mouth.

"That's the way!" Douglas laughed. Then he yelled across the room to the bar. "Keep everything coming for me and my friend."

Twenty minutes later Philip was a changed man. With his belly full of food and beer, he felt he hadn't a care in the world.

"You're a credit to your time, my good man. A credit to your time!" Philip slurred jovially as he slapped Douglas on the back.

Philip took another swig of beer when he suddenly became conscious of an uncomfortable feeling. He turned to Douglas.

"You people have bathrooms, don't you?"

Philip failed to notice when Douglas gave him a look that could appropriately be directed at a flying spider. All he noticed was Douglas's hand pointing to the back of the bar.

"First door on the right."

Relieved, or at least looking forward to being relieved, Philip stood, swayed, then plopped back down onto his seat.

"Think I'll wait for the room to stop."

But the room refused to stop. Even worse, it began to tilt sideways and spin faster. Philip did the only thing he could think to do. He laid his head on the table and closed his eyes until the world decided to act in a more reasonable manner.

As Douglas watched his table partner get cozy for a little nap, he couldn't help but regret his decision to schmooze this man who obviously was unused to drinking alcohol. He'd never met such a lightweight, particularly not one sitting at a bar.

A crowd got up to leave. Douglas looked at his watch and realized that not only was happy hour over, but if he didn't get home soon, he wouldn't have time to write that sales report that was due the next day. No report meant no chance at a promotion. He needed to get home.

As he looked at the pathetic example of a man lying on the table with his cheek in a puddle of Oregon's best brew, something unusual for him happened. He felt an uncharacteristic twinge of sympathy.

This guy most likely didn't have any hidden wads of cash, but he was a nice guy. Too nice to leave here like this.

Having a conscience wasn't very pleasant. He'd have to watch those tendencies in the future. But for now, he'd help this guy.

"Look…" Douglas sighed as he gave in to this rare unselfish impulse. "I've got to work tomorrow. Can I drop you anywhere?"

Philip lifted his head and tried, unsuccessfully, to focus his eyes on Douglas.

"I mean…" Douglas cringed at his own unselfishness. "You certainly can't drive."

"I know," came the slurred reply. "Never learned how."

Douglas blinked several times while he let that bit of trivia soak in.

"You live nearby?"

"Seattle," Philip replied as he pulled himself upright and nodded his head. But the head continued to nod entirely too long, and Philip was forced to slap a hand on each side of his head to stop its nauseating bounce.

"Seattle!" Douglas was surprised. "That's hours away."

Philip donned a goofy smile and raised a finger in the air.

"Hours times infinity," he proclaimed with as much dignity as he could manage. Which frankly wasn't much.

But no, that wasn't right. Infinity was too long.

"Not quite infinity," the very drunk Philip clarified as he scrunched his forehead, "but a long time!"

Douglas looked around at the emptying restaurant and sighed. He might as well chalk this one up to lessons learned and get this guy out of here before the idiot made a scene that got Douglas banned.

"Look," Douglas sighed, "you can crash on my couch. I'm only a few blocks from here."

Philip looked around the room as he swayed in his seat. Not only did he not appear capable of driving, but it was debatable if he could even walk. Or carry a sensible thought from one moment to the next.

Douglas sighed for what he felt must be the fiftieth time and decided to become Saint Douglas for the first time in his life.

"Come on!"

He pulled Philip to his feet and helped him out of the restaurant.

Chapter 4

BY THE TIME THEY reached his apartment Douglas was regretting his generous impulse. Not only was Philip a heavy guy, but he kept singing a weird song that had no real tune.

But Douglas somehow not only managed to get Philip the two blocks from the bar, but he also got him up the two flights of stairs to his apartment.

At his apartment door Douglas propped Philip against a wall and held him in place with one hand as he struggled with the lock with the other. Few things worked as they were meant to in this old building. It probably should have been demolished years ago, but he was glad it hadn't been because truthfully, it was all he could afford.

Until he got his big break, that was. All he needed to do was find the right connections and he would have it made!

The key was finally jiggled in just the right way and the lock clicked opened.

"Good thing, 'cause you've gotten heavy," Douglas muttered at the man who had stopped holding up his own weight blocks ago.

He dragged the near-unconscious man into the apartment and shoved him in the general direction of the couch. Luckily for Philip, the general direction was good enough and instead of hitting any number of hard, pointy objects, Philip landed safely among the cushions.

The jolt dislodged a booklet from Philip's pocket and it fell to the floor.

"Oh no you're not," Douglas muttered. "You're not going to litter my—"

His words of complaint dried up and interest was sparked as the title of the booklet caught his eye.

"What's this?"

He picked up the little booklet and read the title aloud.

"*Department of Temporal Adjustment History Museum*," he mused. "Temporal. Temporal. What—?"

He took a quick look at Philip, who was snoring gently and showed no inclination of waking any time soon, before he plopped onto a nearby armchair. As he propped his feet on the coffee table, he opened the booklet and began to read.

"Time travel was invented in mid-twenty-first century by four sisters. Rebecca, Madeline, Zoe, and Audrey Rossi—"

Philip moaned and shifted. Douglas looked with suspicion at the man sleeping on his couch. But Philip didn't wake.

"What?" Douglas whispered at the sleeping man. "Don't like me reading your brochure? Well, maybe you shouldn't drink if you can't hold your liquor."

Douglas stared at Philip for several more seconds, practically daring him to open his eyes. When Philip declined to take the dare, Douglas continued reading the booklet, this time silently. In case Philip's boozy slumber was shallower than it looked. He didn't want Philip to wake up with the memory that Douglas had overstepped the bounds of propriety by reading something from Philip's pocket.

Douglas was about halfway through the booklet when something caught his eye that was so amazing, so outlandish, that his feet slid off the coffee table and slammed to the floor. The resulting crash was loud enough to wake the dead.

But not the drunk, it seemed. Philip

remained blissfully unaware of Douglas's perfidy as he snored gently on the couch, and equally unaware that he had violated a time traveler's primary tenet by having the brochure in his pocket when he traveled to a time in the past when time travel was still viewed as science fiction.

Unfortunately, Douglas was a cagey one. Most who found the brochure would dismiss it as a quirky example of fiction. But Douglas was a born scammer with an innate sense to recognize a scam when he saw it. And what was fiction, after all, but a form of a scam?

This didn't feel like a scam. It felt real.

He looked at the structure of the booklet closely. It was like no other booklet he had ever seen. Instead of being held together by staples or glue, it appeared to be all one piece. As if it had been created by a technology that, as far as Douglas knew, had not yet been invented.

His heart beating a mile a minute with excitement, he quickly grabbed a page and pulled. When nothing happened, he pulled harder. He kept trying to rip the little booklet for several seconds, even going so far as to put one page under his foot and pull the rest. Nothing he did made even the slightest dent in the booklet. It didn't even look dirty, even though he had stood on it with his dirty shoe while trying to rip it to shreds.

He stood for several seconds looking back and forth from the booklet to the sleeping man on his couch.

"What *are* you?"

Unable to solve the mystery without further research, he shrugged and sat back down on the armchair to go through the booklet at a slower pace. His gut told him this brochure was the answer. He wasn't exactly sure what the question was, but he planned to study this strange booklet like he'd never studied any textbook in school.

As he sat in the chair, perusing the booklet, he found himself looking up every so often to make sure Philip was still passed out. It wasn't that Douglas had qualms about borrowing other people's stuff without their permission. He simply didn't like getting caught doing it. People rarely could see why he did what he did from his point of view. It made for awkward situations.

The more he read, the more interested he became. If this were true…

But it couldn't be true! People couldn't travel through time. It wasn't possible. It would never be possible. It would take—

He turned the page and found an intricate diagram of a machine labeled as the first time travel device.

"I don't know if I believe in all this time travel mumbo jumbo—"

He flipped the brochure over several times, then stared at Philip's odd clothing.

"But if it's true—"

He sat there for a full five minutes as the wheels of his brain turned, and his face ran the gamut of emotions as a full assortment of scenarios played out in his head. Then an excessively devious smile sprouted on his lips.

"Why not!" he shouted. But when Philip groaned and turned, he lowered his voice to a whisper. "I can be an inventor. People would believe that."

He jumped to his feet and paced back and forth as he turned to the page that contained information about the Rossi sisters.

"Might need to do something about you. Wouldn't want you to get any ideas."

He looked around the apartment. A small bookshelf caught his eye and he snapped his fingers and snatched a book with the title *Women's History* in gold letters on the side.

"Never thought I'd read this again," Douglas muttered as he set the book on the coffee table and laid the booklet on top.

"Let's see what else you've got."

He did a quick but gentle search of Philip's pockets. All he found was a small metal box which contained the picture of a curly-haired woman with a mischievous smile. Uninterested, he snapped the box closed and put it back inside Philip's pocket.

"I get the feeling this investment is going to pay well," he said as he looked down at Philip sleeping peacefully.

Douglas gave a firm nod, picked up the textbook and the booklet, and retreated into his bedroom. He wanted to plot and plan without the risk of waking the time traveler who continued to snore gently on his couch.

Chapter 5

THE NEXT DAY—AND a thousand or so years in the future—Philip returned to his own city, and his own time.

Seattle in the year 3027 was gorgeous, clean, and would be frankly unrecognizable to its residents of the twenty first century. Sometime in the past it had embraced its nickname of Emerald City and enacted a program that promoted the planting of greenery of all kinds.

The program became popular, and when new building material was developed that maintained its structure while sustaining plant health, Seattle was reborn as a shining example of what a truly green city could look like.

It was so lush and green, in fact, that it was virtually invisible to satellites. Photos taken from above only showed a wide expanse of green hills and valleys. The only thing that gave away the fact that a city existed in that location were the glimmering lights in the night, seemingly from the plants themselves.

Philip lived downtown in one of the older high-rise buildings that was built before the interiors became spacious and airy, and it really bothered him. He and his wife were expecting a baby and they had a shared goal of being able to afford a better environment for their child.

He opened the door to his apartment and poked his head inside.

"Annabel?"

When there was no response he tiptoed through the doorway and gently closed it.

It looked like Annabel wasn't up yet. Which was fine with Philip. He needed a moment or two to pull himself together. He didn't feel well. Not well at all!

It wasn't just that his breath was decidedly skunk-ish and his mouth tasted like he'd been eating garbage. Everything was off. Even his vision was blurry. He'd stumbled multiple times as he made his way home, and he was pretty sure several of those times the objects he'd tripped over were his own feet.

But the worst was his head. He was pretty sure a creature had crawled up his nose while he slept and was busy remodeling his brain with a blunt instrument. He couldn't even make it to the hooks where he and Annabel kept their jackets without stopping five times to grab his throbbing head.

"Uh!" he moaned. "What was in that stuff?"

When he tried to hang his jacket, his legs decided it was time to sit and the next thing he knew he was on the floor with a broken hook in his hand.

"I've got to fix that," he muttered as he stared at the broken piece of metal in his hand. He laid the hook on the floor and pulled a metal box from his jacket pocket. He opened it to reveal the picture of his wife.

"Botched it, honey," he told the picture. "But not to worry. I'll double check the dates and try again tomorrow."

A quick nod of his head resulted in a groan.

"Best not do that," he muttered to himself, his eyes closed in pain. Then he forced his eyes open to address the photo again. "I will get that job if it's the last thing I do!"

He gazed at the photo and his eyes softened.

"Hope the baby has your smile," he whispered. He gently kissed the smile in the photo. "And those curls."

He brushed his fingers across the curls in the

photo before he looked around the apartment. With a sigh he straightened his back and looked sternly at the photo.

"Why am I talking to picture you when real you is upstairs, you ask?"

He looked at the photo as if he expected an answer, then smiled lovingly.

"'Cause picture you always smiles. Real you is going to be furious."

He gazed at the photo for several more seconds. Then he forced a brave smile on his face, sighed, and snapped the lid closed.

"You'll forgive me. Eventually."

He put the box in his trouser pocket, straightened his hair, pasted a smile on his face, and headed for the stairs.

CHAPTER 6

SOMETHING WAS WRONG AT the Rossi household. Very wrong.

It was a weird kind of wrong. The kind of wrong where the Rossi family didn't seem aware of the wrongness. They went about their daily lives and ignored that everything was...different.

Imagine a giant snow globe. And in this snow globe is the world. Then imagine a giant hand picking up that snow globe and giving it a good shake before placing it on a shelf to settle. Except it's not a level shelf. It's tilted. So even though the shape and size of the snow globe remains the same, as the flakes settle, they land all wonky. Things should be the same—but aren't.

Take, for example, the Rossi living room, where the Rossi family had gathered. There was nothing twenty-first century about it. There was no television, no vacuum, no central heating—just things that would be easily found in the 1920s. Things like a couch, a couple of chairs, an oversized radio, a broom, and a woodstove for cold days.

The Rossi family looked to be virtual Luddites with their complete and utter lack of electronic gadgets. There was no laptop computer tossed on a bookshelf. No tablet shoved between couch cushions. No cell phone left to charge on a table. No router lights flashing merrily in the background. No wireless speaker blaring the latest tunes. No game console shoved under the couch. No…well, no anything! All the modern electronic gadgets were missing. It was as if they had never been invented.

But the wrongness didn't stop with the absence of technology. Even the clothes the girls wore—dropped waist dresses with calf-length skirts—were straight out of the past. No jeans, no sweatshirts. Just handsewn dresses.

Oddly, the Rossi girls didn't seem to mind, or be surprised. It was as if they had grown up in this strange throwback from the 1920s.

And as far as they knew, they had. They had gone to bed the night before in one world and woken up in another. They weren't surprised by this change because it was a timeline shift. When the world changed, so did their memories.

But strangely, Vanessa could remember everything. For some reason, she had retained memories from her previous existence.

Changes to the timeline are funny that way. People accept them with nary a blink of the eye.

Few people worry about things they don't know exist!

Little Zoe certainly hadn't a care in the world. She was on the floor near her mom, teaching Audrey, her younger sister, how to play jacks. She didn't care that the ball had a tendency to bounce off at side angles, as balls made of collected rubber bands often do, or that the jacks were really kernels of popped corn. A game was a game. And Zoe was determined to teach Audrey how to play this one.

"Hey!" Zoe complained as a long lock of hair fell directly on top of her head, blocking her view of the game. She flung the hair off to the side and noticed that Audrey's mouth was moving in a suspicious manner and nearly half of the popcorn was missing.

"Mom, Audrey's eating our game again," Zoe tattled.

"Don't eat off the floor, Audrey. It's dirty," Vanessa said calmly.

"No, it's not, Mommy. You mopped it."

"*Audrey.*"

Audrey looked at her mother's stern face and grinned.

"Yes, Mommy. I'll get a bowl."

Audrey jumped up to make her word good. While she climbed like a monkey onto the countertop to retrieve a bowl from the cupboard, Zoe watched Vanessa chop another long strand from Becca's hair. It was odd to her. She had never seen a girl with short hair before.

"There." Vanessa smiled as she brushed a few errant hairs from Becca's shoulders. "Maddie, you're next."

Maddie climbed into the chair of doom while Becca moved off to the side. While Vanessa pulled Maddie's long hair into a ponytail for that first big cut, Becca reached up and touched her own hair. It was nearly as short as a shaved poodle.

"Mama?"

Vanessa looked over at her oldest daughter. By her face she seemed to think her head had been chopped off rather than her hair.

"It'll grow back, Becca," Vanessa reassured her.

"Are you sure about this?"

"Positive."

Becca still looked ready to burst into tears any second. Vanessa dropped her hands onto Maddie's shoulders and turned to address her eldest daughter.

"You know the law," she gently reminded Becca. "Girls need a male escort to travel. We don't have one, so we have to *be* boys."

Vanessa turned back to Maddie and twiddled with the ponytail to get it as close to the scalp as possible. It would make practically shaving her daughter's head easier. While she did this Becca scrunched up her nose, mouthed the words "Be boys," then shook her head stubbornly.

"Mama, we can't *be* boys." Becca threw her shoulders back, determined to stand her ground.

"No," Vanessa agreed as she looked at her daughter. Her eyes twinkled merrily. "But we can look like them." And then she winked.

Becca didn't know what to think about that

wink. She was confused about the need to travel and uncomfortable with her mother's desire to break the law. Women absolutely were not allowed—

To the background music of scissors sawing through Maddie's long, thick ponytail, a horrible thought struck.

"Mama, what about our clothes?"

Becca had always felt great pride in her hair. She nearly panicked at the thought of all her lovely hair chopped away, for nothing. Her mother had cut off her hair so she could act like a boy and travel, but she only had dresses. Boys didn't wear dresses!

But there was no panic in Vanessa. She sawed through the last complete strand and the bulk of Maddie's hair landed on the floor.

So much for the easy part. Time for a bit of shaping. All the boys she'd seen had short but well-groomed heads. She needed to make Maddie look groomed, not like a girl who'd accidentally had her ponytail chopped off.

"Not a problem." She continued to snip here and there as she talked. "Just get the sewing box. We can—"

"The Johnsons," Maddie interrupted.

"What?" Vanessa asked, so surprised by the confident tone of Maddie's voice that she barely missed nicking her ear. She pointed the scissors away from her second daughter and asked again, "What was that, Maddie?"

"The Johnsons," Maddie repeated firmly. "They have lots of boys."

Then she got excited, leaned forward unexpectedly, and turned. Vanessa had to do some impressive scissor wrangling to avoid a nasty accident.

"A whole herd of them," Maddie continued excitedly. "Somebody will be our size. We can borrow their clothes."

Vanessa pulled Maddie back into the chair and snipped a few strands as she thought. She shook her head.

"No, I don't think—"

"We're talking about the Johnsons, Mama," Maddie argued. Maddie tried to twist around to look at her mother, but Vanessa put a firm hand on her shoulder to hold her in place.

"Mama." Maddie continued to argue her point, but decided to try a calmer manner. "They treat their clothesline like a closet. You know they do."

Vanessa wasn't sure she liked where her daughter was going with this. It made her nervous, tense. So tense that, without realizing it, she began to squeeze Maddie's shoulder like it was an orange needing to be juiced.

Maddie gently placed her hand over her mother's.

"Don't worry, Mama," she said gently, unconsciously mimicking the voice her mother used whenever she needed to calm one of her children. "They'll never know."

Vanessa froze statue still, unsure what to do. She was already uncomfortable that she needed to encourage her children to break the law so they could travel. Now one of her kids was suggesting theft. Stealing!

What if she'd started her children on the road to a life of crime? If they believed she was okay with hiding their identity and stealing, they might—

"Just to borrow, Mama," Maddie interrupted Vanessa's conscience-driven thoughts. She had felt her mother's angst and was pretty sure where it had come from. "We'll give it all back."

"Unless we fix things, then it won't matter," Becca added.

Vanessa blinked at her oldest daughter. Becca had been fighting her about this trip since she'd first proposed it earlier that morning.

"Does that mean you believe me?"

"Maybe?" Becca shrugged.

It was something, even if it wasn't enough. Vanessa sighed.

"Wish you girls could remember how it's supposed to be. Then you'd understand."

Maddie jumped out of the chair—Vanessa again had to do a bit of impressive scissor wrangling to keep from stabbing the girl—and wrapped her arms around her mother.

"I don't need to remember anything, Mama," Maddie said as she squeezed tight. "I believe you!"

The glare that Becca gave Maddie should have cowed her, but Maddie was made of sterner stuff. She rarely showed it, but she was every bit as stubborn as her older sister. And for the moment, all she wanted to do was support her mother.

Becca could glare all she wanted. The more Becca glared, the harder Maddie squeezed.

The battle of the stubborn sisters might have continued for all eternity if Becca hadn't had a sudden, horrible thought.

"Mama?"

"Yes, sweetie?"

"You're sure this will save Daddy?"

Vanessa's heart skipped a beat at the fear and pain on Becca's face. At times Becca acted so grown up it was easy to forget she was only twelve. Still very much a child.

Vanessa pulled Becca into the hug.

"Oh, Becky-girl!"

"'Cause we need Daddy," Becca whimpered into her mother's sweater. Becca's voice sounded small and fragile, and Vanessa knew it reflected how the child felt.

Vanessa wanted to be able to tell her daughter that everything would be okay. She wanted to say, and to truly believe, that all they had to do as take one little trip to the future, then *bam*, all would be good.

As if this trip was going to be easy!

But instead of pouring soothing words on her daughters' troubled worries she gave them both a good squeeze, then guided Maddie back to the chair. She breathed a sigh of relief as she snipped several strands of hair with no more questions being asked.

Maybe there'd be no more questions. Maybe she could keep all her worries and concerns to herself. Maybe—

"Mama...you never answered me," Becca's voice was calm, strong, and oddly mature for a twelve-year-old.

"I know."

Becca put a hand on Vanessa's shoulder.

Vanessa lowered the scissors, which she was about to use to trim the hair around Maddie's right ear, and turned to Becca, sighing.

Vanessa shrugged. "Traveling to the future, to the DTA, it's all I can think to do. We've got to go to the experts. They'll know how to fix the timeline."

"And Daddy won't have an accident? They'll save Daddy?"

"They have to." Vanessa had turned away to resume cutting Maddie's hair, so Becca couldn't see the firmness of her chin.

"Mama?" Maddie put a hand on Vanessa's arm as she turned to face her.

"Yes, Maddie?"

"What if they don't? What if they let Daddy die?"

Vanessa glared into the distance, and this time both of her oldest daughters could see the granite-like firmness of her chin. And both knew what it meant.

"Then we'll find another way."

Maddie thought a moment, glanced at Vanessa's rock-hard chin, then nodded solemnly. She knew that her mother would do everything in her power to fix the problem that took their dad from them.

Vanessa snipped a few more pieces of hair

before she decided she was finished.

"Done," Vanessa said. She forced a smile on her face before she turned to her third child. "Your turn, Zoe."

Maddie hopped up to let Zoe have a turn in the chair of doom.

Zoe had curls so Vanessa decided to forego the ponytail routine. The scissors closed on a lock of Zoe's curly hair and lopped it off with a loud *snip*.

CHAPTER 7

A LOT HAPPENED IN the next few days. More than could reasonably fit in the few pages available here to tell the tale.

A detailed account of the Rossi family's adventures can be found in *Time Without*. For now, a summary will have to suffice.

The important points are that Vanessa and the girls traveled to the future and discovered that the problem was near catastrophic, much bigger than expected. Not only had some idiot changed the timeline to take away women's rights, but that idiot had damaged the timeline to the extent that in future fewer and fewer girl babies were born until women ceased to exist.

It was a real shocker when Vanessa and her band of little women showed up in a world that not only had no women but didn't even remember that women had at one time existed.

To make matters even more awkward, the DTA itself had changed. Instead of the Department of Temporal Adjustment—that good ol' department charged with keeping the timeline in order—Vanessa and her daughters found themselves in the Department of Tropospheric Adjustment.

Meteorologists are cool and all, especially ones tasked with controlling the weather, not simply reporting it. But compared to time travel...

Vanessa and her daughters did what intrepid women throughout history have always done: They researched the problem, gathered their resources, and made a plan—then headed to the bathroom for a quick potty break before they raced off to clean up someone else's mess and save the world.

It was as they were leaving the bathroom that they ran into Philip. Or, to be more exact, caught him running away. Their meeting was a little dicey and uncomfortable at first—it turned out Philip was the catalyst who had set this whole mess in motion in the first place—but the adults got together and decided that joining forces would give them the best chance to set the world right again.

Not that everyone thought working with

Philip was a good idea. As soon as Becca and Maddie realized the part Philip had played in destroying a perfectly good timeline, they erected a mental barrier that Philip would have a hard time getting past.

He was responsible for their father's death. It was perfectly normal that the two girls had a grudge against him. It would probably be a lot less normal if they didn't.

Unfortunately for the oldest Rossi girls, Philip was an important part of the plan. Whether they liked him or not—and they didn't since they didn't like selfish people who acted irresponsibly and ruined the lives of perfect strangers—they needed to work with him. This story picks up in a warehouse in 1920. How they got there isn't as important as the fact that Becca and Maddie are preparing to head to Nashville to heal the timeline, and their traveling companion was to be Philip.

An onlooker would most likely find the scene strange. At first glance it was a group of guys hanging out in an empty warehouse, the two youngest playing jacks off to the side. But a closer look would reveal that only the biggest guy was a male. The others were not. They were one hundred percent female. Dressed as guys.

Philip had already changed into clothing appropriate for 1920 and slathered on a layer of dirt. The only way the troupe could get from Seattle to Nashville with the resources they had available was by riding the rails. Illegally.

Train-hopping hobos weren't exactly known for their cleanliness, or good health. Since the last thing Philip wanted was to stick out in a crowd, he piled on the dirt to both help with his disguise and hide his robust health. Then he put on a hat and pulled it down low on his forehead.

Vanessa, for her part, was busy adding decorative layers of grime to her two oldest daughters.

She added a streak of dirt directly above Maddie's right eyebrow and added another on her chin to match. She held her child at arm's length and sighed. She'd spent years trying to keep her daughters clean. It hurt her mother's pride to purposefully smear dirt on these beautiful girls, even if it was necessary camouflage.

One final look at her handiwork and she stepped back, satisfied.

"That should do it." She nodded.

She'd done a good job. Not one of Becca or Maddie's friends would recognize these scruffy hooligans as a Rossi girl. Even their own father would be hard-pressed to—

Thinking of Tony was a mistake. As her eyes teared up and she struggled to hold it together, she found she was spiraling down a rabbit hole that managed to skip right over how important this was to the world and straight to the dangers her daughters were sure to face. She grabbed them both and pulled them in tight.

"I don't like this," she whispered.

"Only way, Mom. We'll be okay." Becca's mouth was crushed against her shoulder, so the reply was a bit muffled.

"You'd better be." As she squeezed her children tight, Vanessa sent a glare Philip's way that made him uncomfortable. Suddenly his collar felt too tight and he had to undo his top button to loosen it.

With what must have been the tenth sigh that day, Vanessa kissed her two oldest children on their cheeks and let them go. Or at least, that was her intention. When she tried to let go, she found she couldn't quite release her grip.

So, there she stood, her arms wrapped tightly around her two eldest children, while visions of every imaginable danger her daughters might possibly face flashed before her eyes.

"Maybe we should all go." She looked at the two younger children and bit her lip. "Stick together. I'm sure we could—"

"Mom," Maddie interrupted, "Audrey."

"Audrey's strong. She can do it."

"Mom, she's four!" Becca shoved her way out of the hug. Vanessa dropped her arms, which freed Maddie also.

"And loves to climb," Maddie added.

"We'd barely get two blocks before she was either on someone's roof or needed to be carried," Becca continued, straightening her messy, hobo clothes as best she could.

Vanessa's shoulders slumped. The girls were right. The plan for Becca and Maddie to go with Philip came about because traveling with the two little ones would not only be impractical, but downright stupid.

Still, Maddie might trip and fall. Becca might catch a cold or cut herself on a rusty knife. One of the two might bump her head and lose her memory. Or both. Any number of horrible things that would require a mother's help might happen. How could she allow her precious children to—

"Mom," Maddie interrupted her mother's runaway thoughts. "You don't need to worry."

"We got our memories back," Becca chimed in.

"We remember," Maddie said.

"Plus some," Becca added.

"What does 'plus some' mean?" Philip asked from the sidelines.

Philip immediately regretted opening his mouth when Maddie looked at him like he was a bug she wanted to squash.

"You wouldn't understand." Becca's tone said it all, but just in case Philip was dense she stuck her nose in the air.

Philip knew he'd been snubbed. It was obvious. Vanessa watched him step back several paces and pull at his collar, which, though unbuttoned, suddenly seemed too tight again.

Vanessa bit her lip and made a decision.

"Philip," she politely asked the uncomfortable man, "mind giving me some privacy with my daughters?"

Philip didn't mind in the least. As a matter of fact he relished the opportunity to reposition himself on the other side of the warehouse, as far from Vanessa and her daughters as he could get.

Vanessa turned to her Becca and Maddie.

"I know you're mad at Philip—"

"He killed Dad!" Becca growled. "He even admitted it!"

"No." Vanessa shook her head and smiled kindly at her daughters. "He admitted to being careless. That's not the same thing."

"But Dad died!"

"Yes, your dad—"

But Vanessa couldn't go on. Tears formed quickly in her eyes and spread to clog her throat. She found herself unable to talk. She struggled to pull herself together.

"Be nice to Philip," she said when she finally got her voice under control. "Work with him."

"Why?" Maddie wanted to know.

Vanessa shook her head. Sometimes being a parent was hard work. It required too much thinking.

"If I said, ''cause I asked you to,' would that be enough?" she asked her daughters.

Becca's chin jutted out stubbornly, which told Vanessa everything she needed to know. And when Maddie cut her eyes at her sister and followed suit, Vanessa knew she would have to come up with something better. Something the girls would buy into.

"What if I told you," Vanessa tried again, "we can't do this without him? Would that be enough?"

"He'll slow us down, Mom," Becca answered as her jaw tightened even more. "We'll have to explain—"

"He has a doctorate in time travel theory, Becca," Vanessa interrupted wearily. She didn't know if she had the energy for this argument. "I'm sure he knows a lot more about it than you do."

Becca and Maddie exchanged a strangely mature glance. Maddie nodded. Becca cleared her throat.

"Mom, we need to tell you something."

Vanessa lifted a brow. That glance the two girls had just shared, it wasn't normal. Too mature for an eleven- and twelve-year-old. It made her uncomfortable, like she didn't know her own children as well as she thought she did.

But she'd be darned if she'd let them know that! She could be cool and collected. When she needed to be.

"When we remembered the other timeline," Becca began, "we...well, remembered other things."

Becca shot a look at her sister, then continued when Maddie gave her an encouraging nod.

"Not so much remembered, 'cause we never knew these things before."

"It was like this wall," Maddie added.

"A thick, brick wall." Becca nodded.

"That just...turned to glass."

"We could see...everything."

"Time, laid out in front of us." Maddie's eyes glowed with excitement.

"Mom." Becca faced her mother and stood tall. Her eyes begged Vanessa to accept what she was saying. "We understand."

"*Really* understand," Maddie contributed.

"Time," Becca clarified.

Vanessa nodded as she tried to take in and understand what her children were telling her. Then she had a thought.

"The time maps. That's what you see through this glass?"

Maddie and Becca nodded.

"That's why we don't need Philip," Becca stated flatly.

Vanessa looked at her two oldest children, unsure what to think. What they had just told her was wonderful, and frightening.

Then visions of her daughters as infants flashed before her eyes. She straightened her back and stood tall, suddenly in full mother mode.

"I could care less what you see or don't see," Vanessa stated firmly.

She glared at her two oldest children as she unconsciously assumed the superwoman stance.

"You are eleven and twelve years old. You are absolutely, positively, not traveling across the country by yourselves. Do you understand?"

Gone were the strong young women who had felt a few moments of superiority to their mother. Becca and Maddie were now just kids, and kids in trouble, at that. They nodded meekly.

"Good." Vanessa relaxed enough to smile. "Now give me one more hug and go fix this mess."

Becca and Maddie threw themselves into their mother's arms and squeezed tightly.

CHAPTER 8

SEVERAL DAYS LATER, PHILIP and the girls had become as close to professional train-hoppers as it was possible of becoming. Even sneaking onto freight trains to hitch rides across country became easier with practice.

After hopping onto the latest train, Maddie and Becca had been thrilled when they found a freight car full of pillows, blankets, and boxed goodies destined for a fancy department store on the East Coast. They were looking forward to the first comfortable night's sleep in days.

They'd made terrific time on their cross-country journey. They might even call it record-breaking, except they didn't have even the remotest idea what that record might be. Hobos tend to keep those kinds of statistics to themselves.

Maddie and Becca were snoring peacefully

when the train stopped at a station and Philip was awakened by the distinctive sound of freight cars being unhooked and shuffled to a new train. He stuck his head out of the door, curious what was happening.

No one was nearby and the coast was clear, so he jumped down to check things out. There were sure to be workmen about who knew what was happening. All he had to do was find one who enjoyed the sound of his own voice while he worked.

He actually found several who were having a discussion. As soon as he heard the words "diverted" and "north," Philip scampered back to the freight car as fast as his legs could carry hIm.

"Get up, we've got to go!" he hissed as he shook the girls awake.

It wasn't easy to wake the sisters. They were exhausted from their travels and each of them had eaten a full box of chocolates before curling up on a stack of pillows to sleep. The last thing they wanted to do was wake up and remember the monumental task they still had before them.

"Hurry up! This car is being connected to a different train. If we stay, we'll end up in Canada."

Philip's words finally broke through the pleasant dreams. The girls, groggy and half asleep, stumbled behind Philip off the train. He had discovered that there was another station a mere mile and a half away with a direct line to Nashville.

It sounded easy enough. Except the hike took them through a dense forest complete with an overabundance of thorns that snagged their clothes and scratched their hands and legs. And then there were the roots. Who knew roots could spring up and trip the unwary?

Those things would have been endurable if the heavens hadn't opened up and drenched the trio before they could sprint to find shelter under the dense trees.

Misery didn't begin to describe how the trio of travelers felt before they had even reached the halfway mark.

Then there was the mud. It was the stickiest, gluiest, muckiest, molasses-heavy mud they'd ever had the displeasure to tromp through. It mired their every step and sucked the energy from their bodies as it vacuumed their feet toward the center of the earth.

Soon they were cold, wet, and as miserable as three people could be who were alone in a strange time period with the weight of the world's future on their backs.

Pretty darn miserable, in fact.

When they finally reached the edge of the woods and stepped into the clearing to see that lovely train, peacefully sitting on the tracks with smoke billowing out of its stacks, they felt they were home.

Until the train's wheels began to move. It chugged its merry way down the track—without them on it.

Philip, Maddie, and Becca didn't hesitate even a second. They raced out of the woods, intent on catching that train. Philip, with his long legs, made short work of the distance to the train and was soon grasping a handhold—jogging along beside the train the entire time—as he turned to assist his partners in crime.

But the girls were not men, they were children and couldn't be expected to compete with a grown man. When Philip saw how far behind they had fallen, he let go of the handhold. He would find another spot to board the train. A spot the girls could reach. He scanned the back of the train as he waited for the girls to catch up.

By the time the girls reached Philip the train had gained too much speed to simply climb aboard. Philip used a maneuver he'd perfected several days before: He unceremoniously grabbed Becca, tossed her into the closest car, then did the same with Maddie. As soon as Maddie's feet hit the floor Philip jumped into the car after her.

The train went around a curve as it picked up speed and Philip nearly toppled off the train. Maddie and Becca each used one hand to keep him from falling while the other held on to the wall for dear life. The train eventually hit a straightaway and Philip was able to right himself.

"We'd better go inside, before we hit another curve," he yelled. Becca and Maddie nodded their agreement.

Grumbles filled the air as the newcomers stepped out of daylight and into the darkened car. Unknown to the trio the car they had hopped was already occupied. More than just occupied—it was crammed full of scruffy men.

Maddie nervously grabbed Philip's arm. During their travels they hadn't always been alone, but never had they come across a car this overfull of humanity. One or two travelers at a time was the most they had encountered.

Philip looked around at the bodies strewn throughout the car and turned back to the doorway. This car wasn't going to work. This large number of men congregated in one spot probably meant trouble of some sort. Drifters rarely joined forces like this. This group had a purpose.

He needed to get the girls to a safer place.

He stuck his head out the door and immediately pulled it back in again. It had only taken a second for him to see that there were many more curves up ahead.

"We can't stay here," Philip whispered. "But there's nowhere to go out there. I'm not sure—"

"Philip, look!" Becca whispered, as she pointed at a ceiling trapdoor deep in the car.

Philip nodded. "Let's try it," he whispered.

The trio tiptoed through the minefield of bodies toward the ladder, Philip leading the way. As soon as he reached the ladder he clambered up and threw open the trapdoor. Bright daylight from the summer sky poured in.

Groans from the sleeping hobos filled the air, but Philip couldn't hear it over the rush of the wind as he stuck his head through the opening, prairie dog style, to look around.

What he expected to find he wasn't sure. A solution, maybe, to the overcrowded freight car below.

But all he saw was the top of the train. Miles

and miles of it. And, of course, the ground whooshing past along the sides.

Not the safe path to other parts of the train he'd been hoping for. This wasn't a solution— it was a death sentence.

No, he'd have to find another way.

While Philip thought through possible solutions—his head and shoulders still standing tall through the trapdoor—the bright light poured its warm glow over the sleeping hobos, waking them from their slumber.

For most, this would be a great way to wake up. Except, these hobos had no desire to start their day. They were tired, hungry, and cranky. Not one of them had the life he had planned. The last thing any of them wanted was to wake up and face the fact that this day, just like the day before and the day before that, was going to be filled with struggle and want.

Not one woke with a smile, only with a grumble. And by the time Philip took that first step back down the ladder, the grumbling hobos had formed a threatening semicircle around Becca and Maddie, who held on to the ladder as if they feared drowning in the sea of grumbles.

Not that Maddie and Becca weren't doing their best to look tough. They had their shoulders thrown back and sneers plastered on their faces. But even a fool could see it was all an act. The level of discomfort was too high.

Maddie was particularly close to cracking. She had used every trick she could think of to stifle a whimper that threatened to escape and was quickly losing her grip on her throat muscles. Rarely had she been in such a position as this, with a large group of angry men crowding her and her sister. It made her feel weak and vulnerable, and very, very young.

About when Philip took a second step down the ladder, Maddie thought about how reassuring it would be to have her dad there instead of Philip. Which made tears form in her eyes. Which loosened her throat muscles and allowed a tremendous whimper to escape.

So much for the tough act. Becca threw her a scornful look.

As if in response to that sign of weakness, a huge man in very ragged clothing shoved his way to the front. He grabbed Becca with one hand and Maddie with the other and tried to pull them away from the ladder, but Becca was more tenacious than that. She held on to the ladder like a leech, until the man finally decided there was a better way and let go of both girls.

"You don't belong here," the big hobo

growled, his face so close that the two girls were overwhelmed by the putrid combination of onions and rotting teeth. "There's no room. Move along."

Becca crossed her eyes and looked at her sister, causing Maddie to giggle. This angered the big hobo even further and he growled like a tiger, which unfortunately sent more bad breath toward the girls and they immediately broke out in a fresh set of giggles.

This hobo, as big and menacing as he was, had a flaw: He hadn't been around children since he was a child himself and didn't know that if a child giggles during a threat, that threat becomes null and void. Those were the rules and there was no getting around them.

So instead of creating a new threat, he doubled down on the current threat. He used his thumb to point first up the ladder and then out the door.

"Take your pick which way you're gonna go." He lowered his brows and speared the two children who dared to enter his domain with his eyes. "But make no mistake, you're gonna go."

Becca rolled her eyes, reached up, and tugged on Philip's trousers. Philip looked down and groaned.

"This can't be good," he grumbled.

"Not good" was an understatement. He could see that an angry mob of hobos had the girls surrounded. Whether they were upset that they had been woken or offended that anyone would dare to step into their den he wasn't sure.

But he was sure they were intent on violence. Several of the closer hobos were staring intently at the girls as they punched tightened fists into palms, threateningly.

Philip immediately took action and jumped down the ladder to put his body between the two youngsters and the mob.

"You okay?" he whispered to Becca and Maddie. They nodded that they were fine, and he motioned to the ladder. "Go. But be careful."

Maddie and Becca weren't as afraid as they should have been, but they weren't stupid. They scrambled up the ladder and through the trapdoor.

Philip straightened to full height, which was impressive, and turned toward the crowd of hobos. He noticed that several of them stepped back, as if intimidated.

"Leave us alone," Philip growled with every ounce of threat he could muster, "and we'll leave you alone."

That was all that was needed. The big hobo nodded his agreement and stepped back. He was a coward and a bully and had no desire to test Philip's muscles against his own.

Philip sent one last warning glare around the car and climbed the ladder. The hobos watched as he exited to the roof and didn't look away until Philip had slammed the trapdoor closed. As darkness returned to the car, the hobos returned to their sleeping spots to go back to sleep, out of the light and out of the story.

CHAPTER 9

"HEY!" BECCA SHRIEKED.

The trapdoor had slammed closed, barely missing her foot. She did what anyone who disliked pain would have done—she jerked her foot away from the trapdoor as quick as she could. Which, unfortunately, caused her to lose her balance. If Philip hadn't had such great reflexes and grabbed her before she tumbled off the roof of the train, this would have been a much shorter story.

"Careful!" Philip admonished as he steadied Becca on her feet. "Your mother would kill me if you fall off this train."

There was no trace of thankfulness in the glare Becca sent Philip's way. As a matter of fact, if the expression on her face was any indication, Becca placed the blame of the three of them teetering on top of a moving train firmly on his shoulders.

He could almost hear her thinking that if something bad happened, Philip would deserve every punishment he got. And the more the better.

"She's not going to be awfully happy even hearing we were up here," Maddie shouted. She was shouting not out of anger—though she did become overwhelmed by anger whenever she thought about her dad's death—but because yelling was the only way she could be heard. The roof of a moving train was not exactly quiet.

"Maybe you shouldn't tell her?"

Becca lowered her brows menacingly. "Whether we tell her or not depends on how good you are at taking orders."

Philip looked from one glaring face to the other and sighed. It was obvious the Rossi girls hadn't forgiven him for the part he played in breaking the timeline.

He wondered how long it would take for the girls to let go of their anger toward him.

Might be a while, he decided. He was pretty sure the adult in the group needed to learn how to forgive before the children would. And he was a long way from forgiving himself.

Best to get back to business.

"We need to find a better place," he said as he scanned the train. "This doesn't seem safe."

They were near the back of the train, so Philip decided their best bet was to go toward the front. As he cautiously stepped to the edge of the car to evaluate what dangers they would face, he heard a strange scuffling noise behind him. He looked down to find Maddie and Becca had crawled on their hands and knees to join him at the edge.

The relief he felt was immense! With all their big talk of being in charge, the girls still needed his help. And they knew it.

Theoretically, that should make working with them a little easier.

He looked across the gap between the cars and his heart plummeted. They'd never make that jump. The distance was huge!

Then his eyes were drawn to the place where the cars were hooked together. That gap was much smaller. They had options.

Philip turned around and scooted to the edge so he could lower himself, feet first, off the roof of the car. But before he could get far he was stopped by a hand on his arm.

"What are you doing?" Becca asked, panic evident in her voice and face.

"We'll never make the jump from up here. We have to go lower," Philip explained. He kept his voice calm and level to ease the child's fears.

Becca looked across the gap, then nodded. But she didn't let go of Philip's arm. "Isn't it dangerous, climbing around on a moving train?"

"I'd say so."

Becca looked at the scenery zipping by, then at her sister, who had a death grip on her leg and showed no sign of letting go.

Maddie was holding it together, but just barely. "Isn't there another way?"

"None that I can see."

Becca blinked rapidly several times as her brain processed the facts of the situation. She took another look at her sister, then came to a decision. Her jaw hardened with resolve.

"Lead on, Philip," she commanded before she released his arm and turned to pry Maddie's hand off her leg.

Philip nodded, looked for the best handholds, and made his way off the roof. It only took a few seconds after his feet touched bottom for Becca and Maddie to cautiously follow suit.

He looked at the girls' frozen faces. It was obvious they were scared witless. But there was nothing for it. Scared or not, the three of them needed to get to a safer location.

"We've got to keep moving," Philip yelled.

As soon as Becca and Maddie nodded their agreement, Philip steeled up his courage and jumped. His long legs had no problem crossing the gap and he landed safely on the other side.

"It's not bad," he encouraged as he leaned across the divide and held out his hand. "Come on!"

As Becca eyed the distance and mentally calculated the trajectory she needed, Maddie did the unexpected. She flattened herself against the car.

"You first, Becca."

Becca looked at her sister doing a very good imitation of a bug on a windshield and shook her head.

"No, you."

"You're older."

"I'm not going first, Maddie," Becca explained with a firm shake of her head. "You'll chicken out."

"Already have." Maddie stared, mesmerized, at the ground whizzing by. She turned a face frozen with fear to Becca. "I can't do it."

"Sure you can," Becca assured her. "It's like climbing trees. You like to climb trees."

"I've never climbed a tree going sixty miles per hour."

"We're going faster than that!" Becca joked, hoping humor would be the catalyst that broke through her sister's paralyzing fear.

"I'll stay here," Maddie said, her chin jutting out stubbornly.

"You can't stay here."

"Why not?"

Keeping her back firmly against the wall of the car, Maddie slid down until she was in a sitting position.

"I'm comfortable."

Becca blinked as her brain worked frantically. Maddie usually followed her lead and did as she asked. Unless something pushed her into a stubborn mood. Then she was harder to reason with than any person Becca had ever met.

"The train people will see you," Becca argued. "They'll kick you off."

"I'll be small."

Maddie curled into a ball and made herself as small as possible. Philip, watching, jumped back across.

"You'll roll off as soon as you fall asleep," Becca pointed out.

Maddie's hand snaked out and grabbed hold of a heavy metal bar that was securely attached to the train. Becca rolled her eyes.

"What's going on?" Philip asked.

"She's afraid to jump," Becca explained as she pointed to her sister who had somehow managed to squish herself against the wall of the car while tightly curled into a little ball.

"Afraid to fall!" Maddie yelled.

"I should have come by myself," Philip muttered as he shook his head in disgust. "How hard is it to make sure a letter gets delivered? By now I probably could have—"

"What did you say?"

Becca had heard every word and was offended. But she knew that if Maddie continued to act like a scared baby instead of a mature young woman, they would never get their mission accomplished and Philip's point would be proven valid.

"Nothing," Philip muttered.

Becca might still be a child, but she had learned how to intimidate her sisters years ago and used that knowledge on others when necessary. The glare she turned on Philip made him feel as if he was a mosquito that had hitched a ride in her space capsule.

After Philip was successfully cowed, Becca turned her attention to the problem of her sister. A stubborn Maddie had to be handled with care. She needed to find something that would motivate her sister. Something—

Becca turned away from her sister and smiled to herself. Then she wiped away that smile as she bent over and whispered in Maddie's ear.

Maddie stiffened.

"What's happening?" Philip asked.

"Sister talk."

Becca studied Philip, which made him fidget—Philip never knew what was going on in that brain of hers—before she whispered a few more sentences in Maddie's ear. Whatever she said made Maddie uncurl and send her own monumental glare Philip's way.

"Becca…" Philip's discomfort skyrocketed as he realized pure hate was bombarding him from the eleven-year-old's eyes. "Maybe I could—"

Without looking his way, Becca lifted a palm. Philip fell silent. Whatever Becca's plan to help her sister, he was to have no part in it.

Becca thought for a second, then continued

with the whispers. Maddie nodded in response, stood, and ramped up the power of her glare to astronomical proportions.

"Maddie…" Philip attempted a placating smile. "Take my hand. I can help—"

Maddie raised her chin and turned away from Philip, who fell silent. It was obvious his help was not wanted.

Without another word the two girls joined hands and jumped across.

Philip, confused, waited for a few seconds, then followed.

"Maddie," Philip said as quietly as he could and still be heard over the sound of the train, "if you need help, just ask. I'll help. We might have to do this quite a few more times before we find a place."

"I'm practically an adult. I don't need your help," Maddie answered, her chin again jutting skyward.

The car in front of them had a ladder to the roof, so Philip put a foot on the bottom rung before he turned to study the two girls. He sighed.

"I know you hate me, but I'm trying to make things right."

Philip climbed the ladder. Maddie sent a questioning look to Becca, who shrugged.

Maddie did the only reasonable thing she could. She followed Philip up the ladder.

CHAPTER 10

THERE ARE MANY TRUTHS IN the world. Like how the one day you oversleep will be the day your usually milk-hating husband makes a smoothie that uses the last of the milk and you have to scramble eggs for your kids while scrambling to get dressed. Or when you finally get an assigned parking spot at work, it's the one under a tree that houses a flock of birds. Or that when you're offered the job of your dreams it's across the country, which would require uprooting your entire family and asking your husband to give up the job of *his* dreams.

But not all truths are awkward or inconvenient. One of the best and most interesting truth is that every child is adaptable to one degree or another. Some can even be called crazy adaptable. Those are the ones who have brains that are so pliable and squishy that they seem almost inhuman.

Becca and Maddie were two such children.

The sisters crawled along behind Philip for a few freight cars when a miracle occurred. Their fear of heights simply melted away.

Philip didn't notice because he was too caught up in his own thoughts. Not only did he need to find a safe place to finish the trip, but then he needed to plan what they would do once they reached Nashville.

As Philip climbed onto the roof of the eleventh car, or maybe it was the twelfth, he realized he hadn't seen the girls for several minutes. His heart skipped a beat as he pictured Becca tripping and falling off the roof, leaving Maddie cowering in fear, sobbing inconsolably.

Those two poor little girls. They had been protected and looked after their whole lives, only to have all those protections whisked away. This situation must have them scared—

"Tag!" he heard Becca yell. He turned to see her tap Maddie on the arm and giggle as she swooped past her sister. Maddie returned the giggle and ran full tilt toward the side edge of the car. Philip's breath caught in his throat. She'd go over and he was too far away to help her. It'd be his fault—

With a natural acrobat's instincts Maddie swiveled at the edge, took a sidestep, and executed a neat forward roll that brought her directly in front of Becca.

"Tag!" she yelled gleefully as she sprang to her feet and tagged her sister's shoulder.

"I liked it better when they were scared," Philip muttered.

He was happy the girls were okay, and even more happy that his lungs had begun to work properly again. He glanced toward the girls only to find feet bouncing about in the air. He looked closer and was horrified to realize they were walking on their hands—on the roof of a moving freight car!

"I need to find a place, fast," he muttered, "before they kill themselves."

He climbed to the next door and opened the trapdoor to look inside, just as he had done a dozen times before.

Only this time Philip sighed in relief. This car would be perfect. Enough room that they could be comfortable, but not so much the girls could get into trouble.

But the most important thing this car had was a complete lack of hobos. Every car he'd checked so far had been occupied by more than one of them, but none of them had been glad to see him.

Until this car. No hobos. They would have the car to themselves.

Thank goodness the girls wouldn't be able to fall over the edge in an enclosed space like a freight car. The sooner they got to a safer place, the better.

Then he could devote his time to coming up with a plan for when they reached Nashville. He hoped the girls could keep up—

"What did you find?" Maddie asked.

Philip jumped, then looked up to find both girls standing directly in front of him. How did they—?

"Anything interesting?" Becca asked.

Philip pulled himself together and pointed to the open trapdoor.

"Our new home," Philip said with what he hoped was a friendly grin.

Becca bent over to look through the trapdoor. Based on the grimace on her face she was none too happy.

"Let me see," Maddie said as she practically shoved her sister out of the way so she could thrust her head through the trapdoor.

"Wow!" was all she said before she disappeared through the opening and scampered down the ladder.

Becca stuck her head through the trapdoor to check on her sister. Then, sitting back on her heels, she glared daggers at Philip.

"What did I do?" He was surprised that the two sisters had such different reactions to the car. "This is the first one I've found that wasn't occupied."

"It *is* occupied," Becca grumbled.

"Only by a horse. No hobos."

Philip studied Becca's face for a few moments, confused. This car was infinitely better than the one filled with pigs, or cattle, or—worse still—stinky, grumbling men.

He bent over and stuck his head inside. After a quick look his shoulders relaxed and he turned a smiling face to Becca.

"Your sister seems to be happy."

"She would be."

This confused Philip even more. Until he realized that whatever he did would not be enough—could never be enough. Not when he had caused the death of this child's father.

"If you really don't like it," he sighed, "we can keep looking. I just thought..."

Philip left the sentence unfinished. Becca made a quick face at him to show her displeasure before climbing through the trapdoor and down the ladder, grumbling all the while. Philip climbed in after her, happy to get off the roof of the speeding train.

Even though one sister wasn't happy, it still felt like a win.

Becca reached the floor of the car and looked for her sister. As she suspected, Maddie was totally enthralled by the horse. Her younger sister had always loved horses but had never had the opportunity to be this close to one.

Maddie cooed at the horse—even Becca had to admit that it was a beautiful animal, even if it was huge—and gently stroked the horse's nose with one hand as she fed it a carrot with the other.

"Where'd you get that carrot?" Becca asked.

"Over there." Maddie pointed to a locker against the wall. Becca kept as far away from the horse as possible as she moved to the locker to explore its contents. After a quick look she smiled.

"Philip, we've got lunch," she yelled over her shoulder.

Philip was busy arranging some clean hay from a bale into a place to sleep for the night, but he took time to join Becca at the locker. His smile matched hers when he saw that the locker was filled to the brim with carrots, apples, and bags of uncooked oats.

"I may change my mind about horses," Becca said as she looked at the abundance of food. She picked up a fat apple and took a bite. Juice dripped down her cheek with that first heavenly crunch. Suddenly, the day was a brighter one.

"Come over here, Becca. Say hi to Katie," Maddie called to her sister. "It's the least you can do if you're going to eat all her apples."

"I'm not going to eat them all," Becca grumbled. "I'm sure she can spare one."

"Come on! Come have a chat with Katie."

"Katie?"

"Her blanket says KD." Maddie pointed to a blanket thrown across the animal's back. "But Katie sounds better."

"Katie, sounds friendly."

"Oh, she is!" Maddie laid her forehead on the horse's forehead. The horse flicked an ear. "Come pet her!"

"That's okay, Maddie. I'm fine here."

Becca crunched another bite of her apple and stood her ground. Horses were huge, smelly creatures. She'd keep her distance.

Maddie gave the horse another pat on the forehead before she stepped away. She turned to her sister.

"Oh, yeah. I forgot." She smirked, then continued in a singsong voice as if she was reciting a lesson from school. "You don't like horses. Or any animal that might get you dirty."

Becca lifted her chin in the air and tried to flick her hair over her shoulder. Only, her normal long silky hair had been cut short. Her chin dropped as she took in her own clothing, then she gave a long sigh.

"That horse is probably cleaner than me," she muttered.

Not one to give in too easily, Becca threw back her shoulders, grabbed a few apples, carrots, and a small bag of oats, and stomped angrily to the corner where'd they'd pass the night. Philip followed suit, only without the angry stomping.

As Philip bit into an apple, this one green but just as juicy, his eyes strayed to Maddie. As he watched her with the horse it brought a gentle smile to his face.

"Annabel loved animals, too. She was always bugging me to get a pet."

"Your wife?" Becca asked. She used her sleeve to wipe a particularly robust stream of apple juice from her mouth, something she would never do if her mother was around.

Philip nodded.

"Are you gonna?" Becca asked. "Get a pet, I mean, assuming we fix things and you get your wife back."

Philip dropped his head, as if sad, which made Becca's jaw tighten in anger.

"Don't try to make me feel sorry for you," she growled. "I won't. You made this mess."

She threw her arms out as if to encompass more than just the freight car, but the entire world. The gesture was lost on Philip. He was distant in thought as he stared at a single piece of straw on the floor.

When Philip failed to respond, Becca's anger boiled over.

"You killed my father!" Becca hissed, not caring that several apple pieces flew out of her mouth along with a spray of apple juice. "You deserve to lose your wife. It's what my dad would have called just punishment."

Philip drooped even more, if that were possible. Then his head moved the slightest amount as he nodded his agreement. Becca waited for him to look at her so she could give him a withering glare, but he avoided that particular punishment. It was more than he could handle at the moment.

"Besides," Becca continued, determined to make Philip understand how much his actions had hurt her, "it's much worse to lose a father than a wife. You can remarry. But a dad...a dad is blood!"

Philip allowed Becca's hate to wash over him like the tidal wave of anger it was. He deserved it. He had been an idiot to travel back in time like he had, and he had been a double idiot to lower his guard while there. He had been selfish, and stupid, and now everyone had to suffer the consequences. These girls—

Philip raised his eyes in an effort to see Becca, but he might as well have been blind. The river of tears flowing from his eyes made the whole world blurry and out of focus.

Becca sat back in shock. She'd never seen a grown man cry before. She hadn't even known it was possible. She thought crying was something young people did, and that all the emotions dried up in old people, along with the tears.

"I love Annabel with every fiber of my being," Philip said savagely, unable to keep his pain hidden any longer. "Don't tell me my loss is less than your loss."

Philip brought his hands up to his head, overcome by an unendurable pain.

"And I lost blood too. Annabel was pregnant," he said, sorrow dripping from every word. "I lost my child. Is that enough punishment for you?" Philip dropped his hands and glared at Becca, temporarily forgetting she was a child trying to deal with her own loss.

But worse was yet to come. Because as Becca watched, Philip's anger dissolved and all that was left behind was pain. Raw, inconsolable, unending pain.

Becca grew up a bit in that moment as the ache she felt at the loss of her father shrunk just enough to make room for Philip's misery.

Most adults call that compassion, or empathy. Becca simply called it awful.

Philip's eyes cleared, and he realized he had just aimed all his pent-up anger at a little girl. He turned his head away in shame.

"I need air."

Philip shuffled to the sliding door and cracked it open to let in fresh air. Then, as he leaned against the wall, his legs melted under him. Before thought could catch up to action he was a puddle of misery. Trying to regain a bit of dignity he pulled himself upright and leaned back against the wall. There he stayed, wallowing in self-pity, with a stiff breeze on his face.

Becca watched the whole thing in silence. Then her chin hardened, which to anyone who knew her was a clue that she had just come to a decision.

The conversation that happened next will remain private to the sisters. But body language can tell its own story.

First there was Maddie's glee when Becca joined her near the horse. That lasted until Becca had talked for a minute or two and it was replaced by a hardening of her chin in anger.

Becca pointed toward Philip and Maddie grudgingly looked his way. A sliver of compassion softened her chin at Philip's vulnerability. She looked a question at her sister and received a whispered explanation in response.

Maddie gazed with compassion at Philip for a full five seconds before she crossed her arms and glared so hard at her sister that Becca took a step backward.

Maddie either would not accept, or did not care, about what Becca had told her. She was not ready to forgive Philip.

She turned her back on Philip and gave her full attention back to the horse.

CHAPTER 11

TO THE OUTSIDE OBSERVER, things were back to normal later that night. The sliding door that kept everything in the freight car in the freight car was firmly closed. Katie the racehorse was happily munching a mix of oats and carrots that Maddie had lovingly placed in a pile. And the drama level had plummeted way down after Philip managed to regain control of himself. He currently lounged against a pile of hay as he watched Becca and Maddie doodle a sketch on a piece of paper.

But that was what an outside observer would see. Because no one who knew what was really going on would ever use the word *normal* to describe this mismatched band of time warriors. It was not normal that the man had been born a thousand years after the two children. It was not normal that the preteen children were in charge. And hopping freight trains in 1920 to travel across the country to fix a glitch that had decimated the timeline—without a workable plan...still not normal.

Least normal of all was the drawing the girls were creating. Again, the outside observer might think it was merely a doodle.

But it was more, so much more.

It resembled a star chart, but more complicated. Odd lines, both wavy and straight, radiated through the diagram in a manner that made it clear they were important.

Maddie drew a final line and looked at her sister. Becca nodded her agreement.

Becca picked up the diagram, Maddie grabbed it back. There was a stare-down between the sisters. But older-sisterhood won out and Maddie grudgingly released the diagram. Becca immediately handed it to Philip.

Philip studied the complicated diagram in his hand, thoroughly confused. What was he supposed to do with this?

He looked at the girls, who stood staring at him expectantly. Obviously, they thought this was something he could understand. He'd better come clean.

"Um, thanks girls. But…" He handed the diagram back to Becca. "I don't know how to read this."

"Mom said you were an expert," Becca said accusingly as she took the diagram back from Philip. She tilted her head and studied the uncomfortable man. "Shouldn't you know how to read a time map?"

"We told her we'd have to always be explaining everything to him," Maddie grumbled.

"Give him a chance. He's trying to help us fix things."

"And look what happened the last time he 'fixed things.'" Maddie raised her fingers high in the air and made air quotes.

"Now, wait a minute!" Philip stuck a hand between the two girls to get their attention, but they ignored him rather like they would have ignored an annoying younger sister.

"We can do this by ourselves," Maddie argued. "We don't need him."

This argument struck a chord in Becca and she stopped to study him for several moments. He obviously didn't stand up to her standards.

"Maybe she's right," Becca said to Philip. "We don't need you."

It was not easy for a grown man to be told by a couple of children that he was worthless. His ego was bruised. But he knew he had to be a part of the solution, so he pushed away the hurt and stood up for himself.

"Don't need me?" he asked with a well-timed brow raise. "Like you didn't need me with the hobos in that other car? Is that what you mean?"

That shut them up. Particularly the brow raise, which reminded both the girls of their mother.

But brow raise or no brow raise, Maddie wasn't ready to give up yet. She pointed to the time chart.

"You can't read a time chart, right?"

"No. I never—"

"Then what good are you?" Maddie kicked hay all over Philip, which didn't exactly make him happy.

"Whoa, whoa, whoa," Philip yelled, sputtering a bit on the last "whoa" as he accidentally inhaled several straws of hay.

Katie the horse snorted at the well-recognized word and stomped her foot three times. Philip was speaking her language. It was boring having to stay in this freight car all day; she wanted to be a part of the conversation.

Becca and Maddie glanced at the horse. Philip took advantage of the distraction to gently take the diagram from Becca's hand and lay it on the floor between them.

"In my time, time charts are rare, a part of ancient history," Philip explained. "It's not something I would have learned. Teach me. I'm a quick learner."

Becca raised both eyebrows at Maddie and wiggled them several times. Maddie bit her upper lip in response.

Philip, not able to read this secret sister sign language, couldn't tell if his words were doing any good. He decided a little begging couldn't do any harm.

"Please?" Philip poured every ounce of humility he could muster into his words. "You've got to give me a chance to help. I promise, I'll follow your lead."

Philip watched as Maddie and Becca's eyes connected. There were no blinks, no nods, no facial expressions whatsoever. It was more like a data exchange. Philip had never seen anything like it. When all this got cleared up— *if* all this ever got cleared up—he would make sure a study was done about sibling communication. Maybe—

Maddie slapped her hand onto the diagram,

making Philip jump.

"We're in charge?" Maddie's glare hadn't lessened any, but Philip was encouraged. He gave a firm nod.

"You are in charge."

Maddie nodded and a smile, actually aimed at Philip, spread across her face. He breathed a sigh of relief.

Becca and Maddie focused on the diagram and pointed to different areas as they talked. It became quickly apparent they could read the time map as easily as Philip could read a book.

Philip nodded and leaned closer to the diagram. He relished the opportunity to learn how to read the complicated chart. The only person he'd ever seen use one was his darling wife, Annabel. He'd always been too embarrassed to admit this particular gap in his knowledge and he'd never asked her how to read a time map.

"See this line here?" Maddie pointed to a line on the diagram.

"Not supposed to be there," Becca said, finishing Maddie's thought. The girls often finished each other's sentences.

"That's where Harry Burn votes against ratification," Maddie said.

"Which makes women not get the vote,"

Becca added.

"We know what that leads to…" Maddie brought her fingers together, then outward, like an explosion. "Pow. No more Dad."

"You caused that." Becca pointed at Philip accusingly.

Philip's eyes became soft and sad, but he nodded meekly. He was well aware of his guilt.

Becca squinted at Philip as she noticed the beginning of tears.

"Suck it up, buttercup," she said firmly.

Philip blinked. Why would Becca say such a thing? What did it mean?

"My dad would say that when we teared up," Becca explained to the confused Philip. "It's something they say in the Air Force. It means stop feeling sorry for yourself and do your job, I think."

Philip, wanting to build on this budding rapport, did a strange sort of salute to Becca, then Maddie. Maddie grimaced.

"That's not how Daddy does it," she whispered to her sister.

But Philip didn't notice. He was too focused on the struggle to understand the complicated diagram.

"What's this?" he asked as he pointed to a spot with an overabundance of lines.

"That," said Maddie with relish, "is Mr. Selfish himself."

"He's very busy in Nashville right now," Becca explained.

"He's busy later, too," Maddie added.

"But he starts here," Becca clarified. "This is where he really messes things up."

"So, if we fix that..." Maddie shrugged. Then she turned to her sister and they did their special sister handshake. It consisted of a wrist clasp, a shake, then a slide out to a pinkie shake.

"We'll be good?" Philip asked.

Becca and Maddie nodded.

"I have one favor to ask." In all honesty Philip felt he had no right to ask any favor, but this was important. Too important to let his ego get in the way.

"Whatever happens," he continued when he had gotten the girls' full attention, "please, please, please don't leave me in this time period."

Becca and Maddie, in unison, tilted their heads in question.

"These clothes itch," Philip said as he awkwardly pulled at the collar of his shirt.

Of course, that wasn't the only reason Philip didn't want to be left behind in 1920. But the mood had gotten rather heavy and he wanted to lighten it up a bit.

It worked. Becca and Maddie grudgingly laughed.

CHAPTER 12

THE FREIGHT TRAIN CARRYING the time traveling trio whistled merrily as it chugged through the Tennessee countryside on its way to New York. It wasn't scheduled to make another stop until it reached the city, but that didn't worry our intrepid travelers. They were on this train because it would conveniently pass near Nashville. What else it did they really didn't care.

In the train-hopping business, a near pass was better than an actual stop. Only the ignorant or stupid hobo hopped off at stations. And most of those got caught and hauled off to jail!

Jail was an inconvenience that was best avoided. Not even the best time travelers would be able to stop Douglas Whitfield, Mr. Selfish himself, from damaging the timeline if they were twiddling their thumbs in a jail cell.

Philip wasn't worried about the hop from a moving train. On the trip from Seattle, the three had numerous occasions to practice. Philip had picked it up quickly and Becca hadn't been far behind.

But Maddie, well...Maddie had found it intimidating. The ground speeding below her feet tended hypnotize her and it often took a push from her sister to get her moving again.

To prepare, Maddie had stared at the moving ground multiple times over the last few days and no longer fell into a trance. She was actually looking forward to showing her sister what a good jump she could do.

The departure from the train would have gone off without a hitch but for the horse. Just as the trio stood in the open door preparing to depart, it neighed sadly.

The bond Maddie had formed with the horse was a strong one. Katie didn't want to see her go.

Maddie turned to wave goodbye to her friend. As luck would have it the tracks made a sharp turn and catapulted a surprised Maddie out the door.

Becca didn't even think twice. She grabbed Philip's hand and jumped after her sister.

Directly into a muddy mess. Becca stood to look for her sister only to have Philip immediately tug her back down.

"What are you doing? I need to find Maddie!" Becca yelled as she shook a clump of mud from her hand.

"If they see us, they'll arrest us," Philip explained.

"But Maddie—"

"We'll find her. Keep low until the train passes."

Becca didn't like it, but she nodded her agreement. She stayed low as she crawled through the mud in search of the younger girl. Philip had no choice but to follow.

As they drew closer to the spot where Maddie had been flung from the train, Becca felt panic set in. She couldn't see her sister anywhere.

The end of the train zipped past and out of sight. Becca sprang to her feet, cupped her hands, and yelled in a voice hoarse with fear.

"Maddie! Where are you?"

There was no answer. Her heart beating a

mile a minute, Becca climbed on a stump and tried again, but her voice still wouldn't cooperate.

"Madeline Rossi! Answer me this minute!" she croaked.

There was a faint, unrecognizable sound in the woods. Was that a voice, or an animal scurrying away from danger?

"Maddie...are you there?" This time Becca's voice came out clear and loud.

"I'm here," came a faint reply.

Becca and Philip sprinted toward the sound, or at least, they tried to sprint. The mud was so thick it was worse than running through molasses. They found Maddie about twenty feet away with one leg stuck deep in the mud. It would have been impossible for her to get it out herself.

"What happened?" Becca asked in concern.

"I landed okay. But when I ran to catch you guys I got stuck." Tears welled up in Maddie's eyes.

"I thought you wouldn't find me. I'd be stuck here forever, eaten by wolves, or maybe porcupines. I—"

Becca wrapped her arms around her sister and gave her a big hug.

"I'd never stop looking for you, Maddie. We

follow the 'no one left behind' motto."

Maddie wiped the tears from her face, which left behind a serious streak of mud, and allowed Philip to pull her out of the gooey muck.

While the sisters compared notes on the various dangers they had faced in the last few days—angry hobos, speeding trains, leg-sucking mud—Philip took in his surroundings. He was happy to find that he could see the roof of the capitol building off in the distance.

"That way," he yelled, interrupting a replay of Maddie falling backward from the train into the mud. "We'd better get moving if we're going to make sure Harry Burn gets that letter."

Even after all this time neither girl was ready to follow Philip blindly, which led to another one of those silent conversations that weirdly reminded Philip of computer systems sharing data.

These episodes disturbed Philip. He didn't have siblings and couldn't understand how this non-verbal communication could be possible. It was unnatural, creepy even.

After several seconds the girls came to a consensus, gave a nod in perfect unison, and fell into their signature sister handshake.

The handshake was another thing Philip

failed to understand. Particularly this one, which ended with their pinkies intertwined.

But if the girls were happy, he was happy. Together the three crossed the tracks and headed into the woods.

It was time they were on the move. After all, the world wasn't going to save itself!

CHAPTER 13

THE CROWD GATHERED AROUND the capitol had an agenda.

Two agendas, in fact.

The legislators themselves, men split into two well-defined factions, held the center, most visible piece of real estate. They stood together in physical proximity only—their positions on votes were polar opposites.

The first, larger group of legislators was loud and cheery. They proudly sported red roses in their lapels, a symbol of their strong-held belief that if they stood together, they'd make the silly Nineteenth Amendment nonsense crash and burn once and for all.

The red rose contingency was confident they would succeed. Heck, even a rube could look around and see they had the numbers. The vote was purely a formality.

Standing nearby was a smaller group of legislators. These men were quiet, and strangely nervous. Several of them jumped at every loud noise and one kept looking over his shoulder as if he expected a knife in the back at any moment. Instead of red, the roses in these skittish men's lapels were yellow. Yellow represented the golden hope that the Nineteenth Amendment would be ratified and women would finally get a say in the decisions that shaped their lives.

Surrounding the assemblage of legislators were women in white dresses and yellow roses. These women were supporters of ratification and they picketed with vigor and a purpose. If the Nineteenth Amendment was ratified it would mean a successful culmination of nearly seventy-five consecutive years of struggle. Generation after generation of women had worked for this day. Some suffered beatings, some jail, and others the loss of family followed by social ostracization.

Not one of these women planned to do what was considered the womanly thing—to go home to wait patiently. They had been told their whole lives that they shouldn't worry. That a man would take care of things.

But they knew this was a lie. A quick look at

history showed them that. Now they finally had the chance to take their fate into their own hands. This was their moment. The moment of truth. Come hell or high water, the Nineteenth Amendment must be ratified. Women must be awarded the right to vote!

Not that every female thought woman voters would be a good thing. There were those who adamantly believed the status quo needed to be maintained, that women would only lose out on their quality of life if they entered into the sphere of politics. They were represented on this day by a small group of well-dressed ladies, perfect representatives of the upper echelon of society, who watched the picketers with a sneer of disgust very like the one they aimed at ill-behaved children.

Into this mix of protestors, and protestors protesting protestors, ran Pete, a scruffy boy on a mission, envelope in hand. He paused at the edge of the crowd and looked around, unphased by the melee of adults.

"Harry Burn!" Pete yelled. Yelling was necessary in this cacophony of noise. "Delivery for Harry Burn!"

As Pete continued to call out, a well-dressed businessman in his forties stepped out of the crowd. Pete perked up at once and ran to him.

"Harry Burn?"

The man nodded and held out his hand for the envelope.

Pete almost put the envelope in the man's hand, then pulled it back. There was something about the man, something he didn't quite trust. It would be best to make sure. Keeping his job as messenger depended on him doing the job right. Which in this case meant delivering the envelope to the right man.

"I was told to only give this to Harry Burn." Pete squinted at the man. "Are you sure you're Harry Burn?"

"Give it here, boy," the man growled as he snatched the envelope out of Pete's hand.

Satisfied with the response—politicians weren't exactly known for their politeness— Pete held out his hand expectantly.

"Was to tell you it's very important," he said as he shoved an open palm practically in Harry Burn's face. "From your mother."

Pete watched closely as Harry Burn crammed his free hand into his pocket and pulled out a coin. The boy's eyes lit up as the coin flipped through the air and landed squarely on the formerly empty palm.

"Now, get out of here, boy."

What Pete didn't know was that he had

failed in his job. Although he had delivered the envelope, he had delivered it to the wrong man. The man who had given him such a generous tip wasn't Harry Burn, but Douglas Whitfield. The very same Douglas Whitfield who had been nicknamed Mr. Selfish by our intrepid time travelers, Becca and Maddie.

But by this point, Pete didn't care who had the letter. And he didn't care when Douglas grabbed him by the arm and twirled him around to face the edge of the crowd. He didn't even care when Douglas gave him a push. All he cared about was the large tip he had just received.

"Go. Now!"

Douglas gave Pete a second push, which caused the boy to lose his balance and stagger as he was shoved toward the edge of the crowd. Not that Pete cared. He used the momentum to jumpstart his run for home, his eyes still glued to the coin.

No one had ever given Pete a tip this big, this glorious! Why with this money he could—

Pete slammed into Maddie, who had just arrived with Becca and Philip.

"Hey," Maddie yelled. She grabbed her sister to keep from toppling over and almost took them both down.

Pete grasped the precious coin tightly in his fist and glared at the child he had nearly plowed over.

When he got a good look at him he almost felt sorry for the boy. But only almost. The poor child was obviously one of those country bumpkins who spent the day wrestling with pigs. By the look of him, this poor rube had lost the wresting match, and then had a fight with a bush and several trees.

A twinge of pity tugged Pete's heart and he decided he could afford to be magnanimous. He would be willing to overlook the clodhopper's ignorance of city ways. After all—

The bumpkin chose that moment to look at Pete's closed fist, which held the precious tip. The thought that this oaf might be after his good fortune made all Pete's good intentions disappear in an instant.

"Watch it!" he sneered, determined to protect his hard-earned money in any way necessary. He pulled his shoulders back and puffed out his chest like a rooster, ready to fight the bumpkin. He could take him. Pete knew he could.

Philip noticed Pete's aggressive, ready-for-a-fight stance and stepped in close enough to Maddie that he could put a protective hand on her shoulder. He figured the boy wouldn't pick a fight with Maddie if he realized she had backup.

And he was right. Pete took one look at Philip's tall, muscular form and skedaddled.

Becca ignored most of this interplay as she scanned the crowd for their target.

"See him?" she asked Philip.

Philip, who had been watching Pete leave, turned his attention to the crowd milling around them. After a quick but thorough look he shook his head. Douglas Whitfield was nowhere in sight.

CHAPTER 14

NOT IN SIGHT WAS TRUE, maybe, but only because Douglas's back was to Philip as he stashed the stolen envelope away in his inner pocket. He would wait to destroy it when no one else was around to see.

But he was there, all right. A mere ten feet away.

Douglas Whitfield patted the envelope in his pocket and decided it was time to get down to work. He had the letter, but that was not enough.

He was new to the time travel business, far from expert status. It might be common for time to heal itself. Someone's wife, or daughter, got to one of the legislators he might decide to vote for ratification rather than against. Burn's mother might send a second letter. Or a blight might form on all those red roses stuck in all those lapels and their wearers could come down with a bad case of hay fever.

Stranger things have happened. Like when the schematics of a time travel machine fell out of a drunk guy's pocket right at the feet of the perfect guy to take advantage of it.

No, if he wanted to lock in his place as the father of time travel, he needed to make sure the real inventors never got the chance to invent. Which should be easy since the machine that made time travel possible was invented by a bunch of women.

He'd fix that by making sure the Amendment failed to be ratified. No vote for women, no control over their own lives. Douglas was sure that would ultimately mean less education and fewer opportunities for the "weaker" sex to do things like invent complicated machines that belonged more in the science fiction realm than in the real world.

Weaker sex indeed! Some of his toughest bosses had been women.

It had always irked him to take orders from

a woman. Didn't seem natural somehow.

But he could change that. If he succeeded in fixing history—honestly, women should have never gotten the right to vote in the first place—he would never have to worry about having a woman boss again. Ever.

To do the job right, he needed to be on the inside. In this case that meant getting in tight with these politicians.

Luckily, he was an old pro at inserting himself into groups. And since that's what politics seemed to be all about, he was sure he'd fit right in.

He found a likely looking group of legislators with red roses pinned to their lapels and tried to edge his way in. But instead of making room for him, the men moved closer together, shoulder to shoulder.

He was blocked out! This had never happened before. He had always been able to squeeze into any group. He would slither in, turn on the charm, and before anyone realized he didn't belong, he would have made friends. Then he did belong.

Sometimes the difference between being part of a group and not being part of a group was a single friend. You never knew who might prove helpful, so he made friends every chance he got.

It was a great system that had served him through the years.

Were they purposely ignoring his presence, or were they so caught up in their own business, chatting, laughing, and giving each other congratulatory backslaps, that they sincerely hadn't noticed him?

He stood back and watched the group for several minutes, looking for a way in. He was studying the mannerisms of several of the men—if you acted like one of the guys, you were often accepted as one of the guys—when he noticed that one man looked familiar. It took him a moment, as the picture he'd seen in the history book had been black and white, but then he snickered quietly. The man was Harry Burn, the intended recipient of the stolen envelope.

Burn, a clean-cut freshman legislator, looked even younger in person than he had in his picture. The awkwardness of his stance made it obvious he was painfully aware that he was the youngest legislator in the vote and would have to work to be accepted.

"Imagine," Harry Burn said with a contrived grimace, "women voters!"

Burn was relieved when the men of his

group laughed at his witticism. It felt good to be a member of a group. To really belong and be valued.

"Husband, how should I vote?" the high-pitched voice beside Harry belonged to a middle-aged legislator with three daughters. "This is just too much for my poor little brain."

Harry laughed with his fellow legislators. He respected women and felt uncomfortable making fun of them like this, but he had no choice. He needed to fit in to represent his district properly. A little secret laughter wouldn't hurt anyone.

"It sure would encourage bachelors to get married," a man across from Harry piped in. "Twice the voting power!"

"Probably why the old biddies are pushing so hard!" the man on the other side of Harry added.

The circle broke out in more laughter as each man pictured a bunch of old maids pushing for the right to vote so they could capture a husband.

"They should stay in the kitchen where they belong," a voice from outside the circle interjected.

The entire group fell silent as they turned to give a cold stare at the interloper. Only men who had been invited into the group were welcome. All others would be kept out.

As one, the legislators closed ranks.

"Hey," Douglas yelled, "I'm with you. I just wanted—"

But the circle of men chatted and laughed as if Douglas had never interrupted.

Douglas blinked multiple times, stunned by his rejection. He was sure if he joined in the joking—

A pair of feminine gloved hands landed on his shoulders. Startled, Douglas turned to find an elegantly dressed woman in her mid-forties.

"They won't talk to you," the woman, whose name was Sara, explained. "Too close to the vote."

"But that doesn't make sense. I'm with them!"

"Doesn't matter." Sara sighed. She pulled on Douglas's arm to lead him away from the legislators, but he resisted. "Vote's going to be close. Too close. They're not taking chances."

"Chances?"

"That you'll worm your way into the group and convince some of them to change votes."

Douglas looked at her like she was crazy.

"It's too close. Not worth the risk."

"But—"

Sara shook her head. There was nothing else to say.

Douglas looked at the group of men. All he could see was a wall of backs. Each might as well have had a big stop sign plastered to it, it was so uninviting.

"Follow me," Sara said.

She turned and headed for the edge of the crowd. Douglas, reluctant but ready to shift gears if a new opportunity fell his way, followed.

As fate would have it, the two sets of time travelers crossed paths, close enough that Philip and Douglas's jackets brushed against each other. But Philip was looking in the wrong direction and the girls had never laid eyes on Douglas, so the second easiest opportunity to put the timeline right was lost. The easiest would have been to stop Douglas from intercepting the envelope in the first place.

Point for Douglas, the villain of the story.

Not that Douglas had any idea he was close to being caught. He didn't even know anybody existed who could catch him.

As he followed Sara, he kept a sharp eye out for other red rose groups he might be able to infiltrate, but each of them looked every bit as uninviting as the first.

Tough crowd. He'd always thought politicians were an easygoing group who were always ready to shake a fella's hand. He'd counted on it.

He was feeling a bit down about opportunities missed until Sara reached her destination and Douglas saw who was there.

These were his kind of people. Money exuded from them like fragrance from a rosebush. A whole field of rosebushes, from the looks of it.

This kind of money had some very real perks. Namely power, influence, and prestige.

The group of four was comprised of two men and two women. Sara made the introductions.

"This is James, my brother," she said as she motioned to a man in his late forties. Then she pointed to a woman slightly younger than herself who had a definite family resemblance. "And this is Angela, my sister."

"How do you do?" Douglas shook hands with James and tilted his hat to Angela. He had done his homework on the proper way to comport himself in this time period. Social situations had always been his bread and butter and he planned to keep it that way.

Next Sara moved to a couple with the fresh

dew of youth still on their faces.

"This is Charles, a neighbor, and his wife, Rose."

"Nice to meet you." Douglas repeated the handshake and hat tilting routine with the young couple. Then he turned to James, the oldest male.

"Name's Douglas."

"Douglas." James paused as he mentally evaluated Douglas's well-cut suit and stylish hat. "Got a last name?"

"Whitfield. Douglas Whitfield."

"Whitfield?" He shot a quick look at his sisters. "Got some cousins by the name of Whitfield. Live a couple hours southwest of here. Any relation?"

An alarm in Douglas's brain blared a warning that this was a trap. Douglas decided to play it safe. The last thing he wanted was to be caught in a lie. It would ruin what might prove a lucrative relationship.

He needed to be careful not to push things too far by claiming a familial relationship to these people.

"Not likely." Douglas shook his head. "Just moved here from out west."

James raised a brow in question. He obviously expected a few more details.

"Way out west." Douglas motioned with his arm to a place in the far, far distance. Then he allowed his mouth to settle into his most disarming smile. "The West Coast, in fact."

Either it was the right answer, or the smile worked, because James instantly relaxed.

"In that case, nice to meet you!" James slapped Douglas on the back. "Never liked those hillbilly cousins. Welcome to Nashville."

Douglas cringed at the backslap, which hurt a lot more than he thought it should. He was all for handshakes, but what was with all these backslaps in 1920?

Charles strode over to stand beside Douglas, who stiffened for another backslap. But Charles was not ready for anything so friendly.

"Let's talk politics." the young man crossed his arms in front of his chest and studied Douglas. His body language screamed that he did not trust the new guy.

Which didn't worry Douglas. This was something he'd often dealt with and he knew exactly what to do.

"You mean, this?"

Douglas flicked the red rose in Charles's lapel. Charles blinked, surprised that Douglas would be so bold, but he nodded.

"Well—"

Douglas slipped the rose out of Charles's lapel and slid it into his own.

"I'm in!" he said with a smile.

After a brief stunned silence—stealing a man's lapel flower was rather a bold move on Douglas's part—he was indeed "in."

It also looked like he was in for a round of backslaps from the men—he even closed his eyes and braced for it—but there was a disturbance in the crowd that drew everyone's attention. Douglas quickly took advantage of the situation to move out of easy backslapping range.

The disturbance was short-lived, and the crowd quieted, so the group returned their attention to the business at hand. Sara looked at their new recruit.

"Red's a good color." She nodded her approval at the rose that now adorned Douglas's coat. "Although you owe Charles a rose."

"It's okay." Charles crossed to stand next to his wife. He took the rose she had pinned to her dress and put it in his own lapel. "I've got one. It's good to have another man around. We need to make sure this nonsense is stopped, once and for all."

"Women voters." James shook his head in

disgust. "Why would any woman want to get her hands dirty with politics?"

To illustrate James's point Charles grabbed Rose's hand, which was covered in a pristine white glove, and held it high in the air.

"This," he said as he twisted the hand back and forth so everyone could get a good view, "is the perfect example of a woman's hand."

Rose tried to jerk her hand away—the awkward position hurt—but Charles held on tight. When she jerked a second time Charles shoved her hand even higher in the air, as if to show who was the boss.

Realizing it would do no good, Rose stopped struggling and submitted to the pain and humiliation of having her hand twisted and waved about in the air.

"Yes." Charles made Rose's arm contort in ways no human arm was meant to contort. Then he pulled the hand to his lips and kissed it. "This is womanhood at its finest."

Rose bit her lip. The last thing she wanted was to show she was in pain. Charles would not like that.

"Rose understands what's best for her." Charles looked down at his wife, who somehow managed to wipe every trace of emotion from her face. "Don't you, Rose?"

"Yes, dear." Rose's voice was meek and quiet. This was less the result of her compliance, and more because she needed a massive amount of concentration to make the smile on her lips not look forced. If she could hold the smile long enough, Charles would move on to another subject. Then he would leave her arm alone and she could have a few moments to herself.

"She knows I have her best interest at heart. Don't you, dear?"

"Of course, Charles."

"Clean and pure. Just as it should be."

Charles was thankfully done with the arm and let the poor, abused appendage drop. It fell into Rose's lap like a freshly pruned branch to the ground.

Another disturbance in the crowd drew everyone's attention. Rose took advantage of the distraction to pop her shoulder back into place. She completed this procedure with the speed and precision of a seasoned professional. As well she should. She certainly had been given ample opportunities to practice the self-treatment.

"Yes." Charles draped his arm across Rose's shoulder. Rose's face remained calm and composed, showing no sign of the pain she still felt. "A woman's hands should always remain clean and pure."

CHAPTER 15

THE HAND THAT RAN across the wall decorations in the entry hall of the capitol was far from clean. Not only was it covered with a thick layer of mud, but that mud had dried and cracked until it looked more like a dehydrated monkey's paw than the hand of a child.

But that's exactly what it was, a child's hand. Maddie's hand, to be exact.

Shortly after stepping into the hall Maddie had touched a decoration to see if it was, indeed, raised, then had become fascinated by the feel of the bumps under her fingertips.

"It's just like braille!" she giggled. "Or I think it is. Do you think blind people are supposed to—"

"Get your grubby paws off that!" A guard

spotted the offending hand on the wall and rushed across the room to slap it away from the precious decorations.

"What do you think you're doing? You're getting your filth all over the place!"

The guard grabbed Maddie by the back of her collar and shook her a bit as he lowered his voice to a growl. "Ruffians like you don't belong here."

Philip and Becca, alarmed, hurried over to rescue Maddie from the irate guard. The guard took one look at Philip's dirt, compared it to Maddie's, and grimaced.

"This one must belong to you." The guard held Maddie at arm's length while his nose wiggled about in that odd way they do when their owners want to avoid unpleasant smells. In Maddie's case the smell most likely had something to do with the hours she'd spent in close proximity with a horse.

Philip only had a vague recollection of what a citizen's rights were in this time period, so he simply nodded.

The guard released Maddie and gave Philip and the children the once-over. He shook his head while his face ran through a whole gamut of emotions, from disgust to wonder to near anger, but he kept what he was thinking to himself.

"You here to watch the vote?" he asked Philip, and to his credit he managed to keep his voice civil.

When Philip nodded the guard shook his head and pointed to Philip's clothes.

"You can't come in here looking like that. You want to watch the vote, you're gonna have to get cleaned up."

"We have a right—" Philip began, hoping that they did, indeed, have the right to watch the vote.

"You have the right to watch the vote," the guard interrupted, "not to dirty up the place."

Maddie still stood less than an arm's length from the guard. He grabbed her by the collar, then, in a surprise move, used his other hand to secure Becca's collar, too.

"Hey!" Becca yelled. But he ignored Becca's protest and marched the children to the door. Philip, not wanting to cause a scene, had no choice but to follow.

At the door the guard let go of his prisoners and pointed outside.

"It'll be a while before they really begin," he said, and something in his voice let Philip know he meant business. "Plenty of time to get cleaned up."

"We don't have anywhere—" Philip began, only to be cut short.

"Move it," the guard barked curtly, "before I call the police."

Philip clamped his mouth shut and draped his arms protectively across the shoulders of his young charges. This guard seemed to have reached his limit.

"Don't forget to check behind the ears before you come back. That little ruffian"—he pointed at Maddie—"has a clump of something that might not be dirt."

Philip looked closer at Maddie. She did indeed have something suspicious behind her ear. Maybe that was where the smell was coming from!

"Go on, now," the guard said as he shooed them out of the building like they were a gaggle of geese that had wandered inside. "Git!"

Philip, Maddie, and Becca had no choice but to "git." They reluctantly stepped outside into the sunlight.

"What should we—?" Becca began, but before she could form a full sentence Philip turned her to the right and herded the two girls toward the side of the building. The crowd was thick, too thick to walk side by side. He paused to look at the milling mass.

"Where're we going?" Becca asked.

"To find another entrance," Philip explained.

Becca nodded, grabbed Maddie with one hand and Philip with the other.

"Daisy chain," she explained. "Better for crowds. Lead on!"

Philip led the girls, daisy chain style, through the crowd and around a corner. As soon as they rounded the corner the crowd thinned down to nothing and they were alone.

"There!" Maddie yelled. She had spotted a small door partially hidden behind some bushes.

The three made a mad rush for the door. Philip motioned for the girls to wait as he opened it and stuck his head inside. Then, without another word, he slid inside.

"Should we follow?" Maddie whispered.

Becca rolled her eyes and slid inside behind Philip.

"Guess that's a yes," Maddie said as she shrugged and followed her sister.

The room behind the door was obviously used for storage, and not used often, at that. Old furniture was stacked precariously against a wall and was covered with a layer of dust thick enough that it could be mistaken for felt.

Becca, who disliked dust with a passion,

spotted a corner of the room that looked like it, unlike the rest of the room, had been dusted sometime in the current decade. She went to investigate and found a box of hats.

"What do you think? A disguise?" She picked up a fedora, held it at arm's length, and squinted one eye as she matched the hat to Philip's head.

Maddie shrugged. She'd never been one for hats. But she joined her sister at the box of hats anyway. After scanning the room for possible dangers Philip joined them.

The box was filled with an eclectic array of hats that spanned many decades and social classes. A person couldn't help but be fascinated.

It only took a few minutes until they were coughing and laughing as they shook the dust from the hats so they could try them on their heads. Philip chose a top hat, Becca a newsboy cap, and Maddie decided to go with a cap made in the aviator style.

Maddie then spotted a yellow scarf shoved deep into the box. She pulled it out, gave it a vigorous shake, and tied it around her neck.

"Don't you think that's a bit…" Becca let her voice trail off as she pointed to the scarf and aviator cap combination.

"It's dashing." Maddie shrugged. "I like it."

Becca rolled her eyes. But she knew by the set of Maddie's jaw that trying to talk Maddie out of her headgear choice would be a waste of breath. The girl had made up her mind and that was that.

The girls had always been taught to leave a place as neat as they found it, so they spent several minutes shoving the rejected hats back into the box. Philip used the time to explore the room further and spotted a door on an interior wall. He cracked it open and watched for several minutes before motioning for the girls to join him.

Maddie didn't notice when Philip called her over. She only had eyes for the mountain of chairs stacked against one wall. As she stood fingering her scarf—a scarf meant to be worn high in the air—she contemplated her options.

Becca, not noticing that her sister was distracted, joined Philip at the door and pulled out the diagram. She studied the paper while Philip talked.

"We need to find Whitfield, stop him from getting that letter. Does that thing give a clue where to find him?" Philip tapped the diagram with one finger.

Becca studied the diagram for several

seconds before she shook her head.

"It's after noon, right?" she asked.

"I think so."

"We're too late, he already has it. All we can do now is work on getting it back." Becca sounded very sure of herself.

"But I thought—"

"You thought wrong. This isn't a magic chart that can grant wishes."

Becca noticed the hurt yet confused look on Philip's face and felt a twinge of guilt. She gave a tremendous sigh as she pointed to a line on the diagram. The sigh, which was the type a brilliant professor would give a dullard student, rather offended Philip, though he did a good job of hiding it.

"It's right here." Becca ran her finger along a particularly dark line on the diagram. "This means that before noon, we have a chance. But after noon…"

Becca shrugged.

Philip needed time to think, but his ego didn't want Becca to know he needed that time, so he cracked the door open and pretended he was keeping watch.

It was a good thing for his ego's sake that Becca was behind him or she would have wondered how he managed to see anything with his eyes unfocused.

After he'd had sufficient time to think, the girls would have thought it more than sufficient, he closed the door.

"Change of plans," Philip said decisively. "We'll grab Harry Burn. Convince him—"

What they needed to convince Harry Burn remained unsaid as the mountain of chairs Maddie had been eyeing toppled to the ground with a crash that shook the whole room. Any doubt of what had caused the crash was wiped away as, seemingly out of nowhere, Maddie flew to the floor, rolled, and landed at Philip's feet.

Becca calmly reached down and helped her sister to her feet.

"Well that didn't work as expected," Maddie began to explain. "I thought—"

The door slammed open, cutting off Maddie's words. The guard from before, the same one who had had to work to contain his anger, stood in the doorway, fuming. His face was red and contorted with rage and Maddie was sure she saw steam coming out of his head, just like in cartoons.

With a quick glare at Philip and the girls he turned and motioned for someone behind him to enter.

Three police officers—Officers Hawkins, Roberts, and Bobby—swarmed in like they were auditioning for the SWAT team, which was impossible, since it hadn't been invented yet.

But in they swarmed. They grabbed Philip, Maddie, and Becca with a roughness usually reserved for the most dangerous and hardened criminals imaginable.

"You are under arrest," the guard growled when the miscreants were under police control.

"For what?" Philip dared to ask.

"Vagrancy and..." The guard looked around the storage room, picked up one of the chairs, and pointed to its broken leg. "Breaking and entering."

Then he tossed the chair to the side and growled, "Get them out of here."

Officer Hawkins, who was the oldest and biggest, twisted Philip's arm against his back, and frog-stepped him to the interior door only to be blocked by the guard.

"Not through the hall, they're too dirty." The look of disgust on the guard's face said it all. "Take them that way." He pointed toward the outer door, the door Philip and the girls had used to enter the storeroom.

Officer Hawkins gave Philip's arm a particularly painful twist, jerked him around to face the opposite direction, and shoved.

CHAPTER 16

AS THE POLICE MANHANDLED their prisoners around the corner to the front of the capitol building—Officer Roberts and Officer Bobby had noticed the extreme force used by their senior officer and had naturally followed suit with their smaller, younger, charges—Philip's heart sank to his toes, pulled up a chair, and prepared for a long visit.

The front lawn of the capitol building was a veritable ghost town. That mass of humanity they'd had to daisy chain their way through a mere few minutes earlier was gone.

Sure, there were still a few random protestors and journalists milling about. But Philip guessed that since it was lunchtime, everyone who was anyone would have returned home for some refreshment and time out of the August heat.

Except for the legislators, of course. They'd be inside. Every backslapping, rose-wearing, vote-giving one of them. They had to be in the building this very moment getting ready to vote.

That very thought made panic well up in Philip's throat and he was forced to gulp loudly. It was either that or stop breathing, and he was rather partial to breathing. He had done it his entire life and had no desire to stop doing it any time soon.

Philip wondered how the girls were holding up and tried to twist around to check on them. But Officer Hawkins had his arms twisted so tight they had become sticks that just happened to be connected to his shoulders. He could no longer feel either of them.

His body was not his own. It was a robot body controlled by Officer Hawkins. It moved when and where Officer Hawkins wanted it to move.

Which was straight to jail. And while Philip wasted time languishing in jail the legislators would vote and ratification would fail—and so would he. This opportunity Philip had been given—to fix the timeline, to erase mistakes, and to make everything right again—was quickly slipping away.

As was any chance of getting his wife back. Annabel!

∞

Becca had played all sorts of rough and tumble games with her sisters over the years— princess pirate, restaurant wars, tackle football, and archaeologist versus tomb robber were the first to come to mind—but not one had included having her arms twisted behind her back like this.

Now she knew why. It hurt. But worse than the pain was the powerless feeling of vulnerability it gave her. As the oldest of four she had always protected her younger siblings. She didn't do helpless.

She gave a quick, sharp pull to her right arm, just as she had every few minutes since the big oaf had made pretzels out of her arms in the storage room. She was pretty sure by the point of his elbow that her right arm was closest to his pinkie finger, a weak spot in the human hand. If this was true, she should be able to focus her attention on that weak spot and eventually break free.

Becca gave another sharp tug and felt his finger give way. That he quickly readjusted before she could pull her arms fully out of his grasp didn't matter. Her theory had been proven correct. When the time was right, which meant she could get both Maddie and Philip free, she knew what she needed to do.

∞

Angela had chosen to stay behind while her siblings took Douglas Whitfield, their newest recruit, back to the house for lunch. She wasn't the least bit hungry, but that wasn't the real reason she had stayed behind. It was that old gut feeling she had—something, somewhere wasn't right. She wanted to stick around the capitol a bit longer just in case she was needed.

She watched, only vaguely interested, as three police officers turned the corner of the building, prisoners in tow. Then she noticed the tight constraints and aggressive behavior of the officers.

"Must be dangerous," Angela muttered, her interest piqued. She avidly watched the officers maneuver their charges to the walkway only to find it blocked by protestors eating a picnic-style lunch. As one of the police officers turned to yell at the group for blocking a public walkway, Angela got a good view of the policeman's face and realized it was Hawkins, a career officer whose beat included several of her factories.

She craned her neck to get a better look at the prisoners but could only see the back of their heads. Her interest waned a bit and she sat back when she spotted the telltale dirt and grime of the garden variety hobo.

"Hobos! Must have gotten caught looking for a place to sleep on the capitol grounds. Serves them right."

With nothing else around to draw her attention away she continued to watch as the police marched their prisoners, heads bowed in shame, down the freshly cleared walkway. She noted a large group of reporters nearby and wondered if they would stop the officers in search of a story.

"And there they go!" Angela laughed as the reporters swarmed the officers and their prisoners. "Probably think they can dig up some scandal. They'll be disappointed. Not much of a story, hobos trespassing on the capitol grounds. I certainly wouldn't read it."

"The one in front is a big fellow," Angela muttered as she again craned her neck, interested even though she knew there was nothing of interest, "but the other two are a couple of real runts. Too small to be really dangerous."

One of the officers shifted positions to get a better grip of his prisoner, who looked up, giving Angela a good view of his face. Even through the dirt Angela could clearly see his youth.

"That's a child!" Angela huffed as she slid to her feet. "What do they think they're doing?"

The "they" she was talking about was the police. The police held the common view, a view Angela vehemently disagreed with, that children were adults who had not yet grown to their full height. It was believed that they were fully capable of making decisions, taking care of themselves, and so should receive the same punishment as an adult if they broke the law.

She did a great imitation of a giraffe as she tried to get a glimpse of the idiot adult who had put those two children in danger. She wanted to know what kind of adult would encourage, or even allow—

The tall prisoner turned his head and for the first time Angela got a good look at Philip's classically beautiful features.

"Oh, my!" she gasped, transfixed by the stunning bone structure and flawless skin of the man.

To say Angela had never gasped before in

her life would have been untrue. There was that one time when she had been surprised by an overly productive spider that had covered her entire front doorway in a web, then perched optimistically in the center as it waited for its prey to bumble in. That had elicited a hefty gasp. Especially since Angela was the first to open the door and had almost done the bumbling.

Still, gasps were not the norm for Angela. She had learned long ago how to keep her emotions in check. She was a hardheaded businesswoman. She ran companies, was a mother, led the community. She was as tough as they came.

But that face! It was hard not to gasp at that face. It was so beautiful it hurt to look at it. It really did.

Angela averted her eyes, but before she knew what was happening, her eyes had been pulled back to the man like metal to a magnet. Frustrated, she didn't like not being in control. She decided that since familiarity breeds contempt, she'd familiarize herself with his looks and the fascination would be wither away.

First things first. What was the man wearing?

Unlike other men in the area he was hatless, which gave her an unobstructed view of that gorgeous face. She felt herself being pulled in and gave a little shake. Enough of that.

Regaining control, she thought back to the first time she'd seen the officers escorting their prisoners and realized that the man's head had been covered. He must have lost his hat along the way, which wasn't surprising since his arms were being twisted awkwardly behind his back. Not the best position to hang on to a hat.

She moved on to his clothing, which was cheap, dirty, and didn't fit his frame well. He was an enigma, with those shining good looks but filthy attire.

Although, now that she thought about it, she wasn't sure why she equated good looks with wealth and success. One did not necessarily assure the other.

One thing was for sure. This man wasn't from around here. He would have been noticed. And not just by her.

She looked around. Every woman in the area had her eyes glued to the excessively handsome man.

"No, definitely not from around here," Angela smirked, and her eyes twinkled with merriment. If she had needed more proof that women shouldn't have power to vote, this was it. These women's faces had confirmed her suspicions. All it took was a perfect face and their brains turned to mush.

∞

Becca noticed the effect Philip had on women as soon as his hat fell off. Every woman that looked his way continued to look. It was ridiculous, really.

Of course, Becca knew that Philip was good-looking. Anyone could see that. His features were pleasant and well-formed. Plus, he had one of those athletic bodies that make some women go all gaga.

The women at the capitol had certainly gone all gaga. Most of their brains had shut down.

Becca watched as a fly flew into, and out of, the mouth of one woman. She didn't notice. Which skyrocketed the situation past ridiculous and all the way to embarrassing.

"Get a grip, people!" Becca muttered.

She couldn't understand what all the fuss was about. Philip was a guy, just like any other guy. He hadn't done anything to be good-looking. He hadn't worked for it or studied for it. He had been born that way.

Besides, being good-looking didn't make someone a better or worse person. Her parents had always taught her that that came from the inside. Ugly people can be kind and pretty people cruel.

No, there was nothing special about Philip. Nothing at all.

Except for the time travel bit, maybe. But none of these women knew about that. They just thought he was handsome.

Good thing her dad wasn't here. He was *way* more handsome and athletic than Philip. Shorter, yes, but more handsome. He could beat Philip at a game of kickball with one hand tied behind his back.

These women would have heart attacks if her dad so much as glanced in their direction. All of them, every single one, would fall over dead with a single look. That was how wonderful and athletic her dad was.

Maybe it was an age thing. Maybe when she grew up and became a woman—

"Not me!" Becca vowed. She would never, ever, swoon over any man, no matter how good-looking he might be.

Becca felt a sharp twinge of sorrow as she remembered that unless they succeeded in changing the timeline back how it should be, her father was destined to die young. Too young.

No, she could not let that happen. There must be a way to leverage the effect Philip had on women. If she could find a woman—

At that exact moment Becca noticed Angela.

"Perfect!" Becca whispered. Here was just the type of woman they needed. One that had noticed Philip but hadn't allowed herself to go braindead. She exuded confidence, dressed rich, and was just enough interested in Philip to the useful.

"Philip! Hey, Philip," Becca whispered. Or at least, that's what she tried to say.

She was too far away to nudge Philip, and she didn't think he would hear her if she gave a normal whisper, so what came out of her mouth was more of a yelled hiss than anything else.

Philip heard the strange hiss behind him and twisted his head around to look. He found Becca making strange jerks with her head in the general direction of a woman at the edge of the crowd.

"What are you doing?" Philip asked.

"Flirt," Becca ordered.

"Do what?" he asked, confused. He had no idea what the girl wanted of him.

"Flirt," Becca repeated. She scowled at Philip, frustrated that he didn't immediately run with her suggestion. But when she realized her scowl was doing no good, she schooled her features into a more pleasant expression and nodded toward Angela.

"You should flirt with that woman. She might be able to help us."

The look Philip gave Becca made her giggle; it was so full of discomfort and even a bit of disgust. Unfortunately, Philip didn't think to change it before he turned Angela's way.

When Angela got the full brunt of Philip's disgust and discomfort, she was shocked enough to feel the need to immediately sit. Luckily, the ledge she had been using as a chair was nearby.

Obviously, the good-looking man didn't like her looking at him. Maybe he thought he was too good for her.

Humph! Angela straightened her back and pointed her chin skyward. He was the one being marched off to jail. If she wanted to look, she would look all she wanted.

And if she was frank with herself, she had to admit that she wanted.

Becca saw Angela sit abruptly.

"I didn't say to scare her." Becca rolled her

eyes at Philip. "I said to flirt with her."

"I don't flirt." Philip lifted his chin and stood tall. Then he relaxed and shrugged, not feeling the need to keep up a pretense. "I don't know how."

"What do you mean, 'don't know how'? Everybody knows how."

"Not me. I never learned." Philip was embarrassed to admit such a flaw.

"You'd better learn now." Becca ignored the flush of red spreading across Philip's cheeks. She really didn't care if it made him uncomfortable. "We don't have time—"

"Drop it!" Philip hissed. "I can't do it."

"Yes, you can," Becca insisted. "All you have to do—"

"Ow!" Becca yelled, as an elbow slammed into her ribs. The size and shape of the elbow felt very familiar and Becca turned to find Maddie beside her.

"Why'd you do that?" she asked. Then, when she realized what that elbow meant, she changed the question. "How'd you do that?"

"He sneezed." Maddie lifted her free hand and wiggled it in the air. "I took advantage."

"I didn't think of that," Becca mused. "I wonder if I can get my guy to sneeze?"

Becca twisted her head around to study

Officer Roberts, who didn't look in the least ready to sneeze. Maddie scowled and stomped her foot, barely missing Becca's.

"Don't worry about that now," Maddie whispered in Becca's ear. "I know how to help Philip."

"Well, tell him!"

"Don't want to."

"Why not?"

"Still don't like him."

"Maddie! We need him. We've got to work together—"

"He killed Dad," Maddie said firmly as she took a step away from her sister.

"I know, but—"

"I can't forget that, even if you can."

"Maddie!" Becca pleaded. "I'm not forgetting, I'm just being mature."

Maddie kept her mouth closed and her eyes aimed at her sister.

"You should try it sometime," Becca huffed. She knew snark would never work with her sister, but she was too frustrated to care.

Maddie simply continued to stare at Becca. Becca sighed.

"Mom wouldn't like you being like this, you know," Becca said softly. "She told us to work with Philip."

Becca noticed the white edges of her sister's tightly clamped lips and gave in. Once Maddie got in a stubborn mood there was no getting her out of it.

"Maddie," Becca asked with a sigh, "what's your idea?"

Maddie turned to glare pointedly at Philip, which made him quickly look away. He had strained to listen to the conversation between the sisters and had heard Maddie blurt out those dreaded words, "He killed Dad."

It hurt that Maddie still blamed him for the death of her father, but he understood. He was to blame.

Becca looked from Maddie's glare and compressed lips to the back of Philip's head. She rolled her eyes at her sister's stubbornness.

"Fine!" she huffed. "Whisper your idea to me, I'll tell it to Philip."

Maddie whispered in Becca's ear.

"You mean—?"

Maddie nodded, then spent another minute or so in more whispered explanations, her free hand waving about the entire time.

Becca nodded. Maddie started to whisper more, but Becca pulled away.

"I got it," she told her sister. Then she turned

to Philip, who had turned back to the sisters and now looked on with interest. "Maddie thinks you should look at the lady like you'd look at your wife."

"Annabel?" Philip asked, surprised.

Becca nodded.

"What did she really say?" Philip wanted to know. "You two were whispering for a long time."

"That's what she said." Becca shrugged. "Pretty much. I boiled it down."

Philip wasn't sure if he should take the advice of a little girl who blamed him for her world falling apart. It might be a plot to get revenge.

Maddie correctly read Philip's face and rolled her eyes.

"Suck it up, buttercup," she said as she pointed at Angela. "Just look at her but picture Annabel. Think how much you love her, and miss her, and want to talk to her again."

"I don't know if I can—"

"Just do it!" Becca yelled. She was tired of having her arms twisted behind her back and of her sister's bullheadedness.

Philip stared at the two girls who had been put in his care and sighed. He was responsible for their safety. He had an obligation to do whatever it took to keep them out of danger. He had to make sure they completed their mission successfully.

And not just for the girls. If they were successful it should bring back Annabel. Sweet, wonderful, brilliant Annabel.

He could do this. All he needed to do was think of his wife.

Philip turned his eyes on Angela. He had trouble, at first, with his focus, so he looked a bit like he had a splinter in his toe.

But as a clear picture of his wife's smiling face popped into his head, his eyes softened, and a mix of love and longing washed over his face.

It was a good thing Angela was sitting, because when she saw that look on Philip's face it reminded her of her own lost love and her knees turned to jello.

Not even the sturdy kind, either, that might actually support something. But the squishy kind, like when a favorite dessert has been left out too long at a picnic.

Angela sighed, clasped her hands together, and hugged them to her heart. She didn't even realize what she had done until she heard her sigh echoed by every woman in the area. She looked around and found the look of longing in her heart mirrored on the faces of every woman around her.

Funny thing was, not a single man noticed.

CHAPTER 17

WHEN THE JOURNALISTS HAD finished bombarding Officer Hawkins with every variety of question under the sun—a few had even been about the prisoners in his custody—they loosened the circle and made a gap. Officer Hawkins didn't need a second invitation. He tweaked Philip's arm a smidge higher and scooted through the gap at top speed.

Officer Hawkins had been on the force long enough to know that when it came to reporters, it was best to get while the getting was good. Stick around too long and a whole new set of questions might pop in their heads and then he'd be trapped, possibly for hours.

Reporters were on top of the list as his least favorite people. Right below stinky bums who shoved themselves in places they didn't belong.

Officer Hawkins threw a sneer his prisoner's way. Couldn't the man take a bath once in a while?

∞

Angela watched as the reporters moved away and Hawkins led the good-looking man toward precinct headquarters. Hawkins must have been holding the good-looking man's arms rather tight, because the prisoner's lips were turning white around the edges. In her experience, that was a sure sign that the man was in pain.

She almost jumped up to help him. She hated to see any person in pain. But the reporters were still sniffing around for a story, and they would make it seem that she had either gone soft or had fallen for the man's pretty face.

She was a businesswoman in a man's world. She had to protect her reputation or lose her ability to lead.

With a sigh, Angela decided it was time to head for home. She wanted to change her clothes and get a bite to eat before the legislators got down to the business of putting the last nail in the coffin of the Nineteenth Amendment. It was time the nonsense of women voting was rejected once and for all and everyone could get back to the business of living.

She had just slid off the ledge when she heard a child's voice yell, "You're hurting me!"

Angela's head snapped up and she searched the crowd. The only children she could see were the prisoners. She looked closer and realized that their arms were also being held tightly behind their backs. A quick look at their faces confirmed her fear. These children were in pain.

She might not be ready to risk her reputation for a strange man, but children were a different story.

"Stop!" Angela yelled. She quickly straightened her skirt and headed on an intercept course. "What are you doing?"

At the sound of her voice Officer Hawkins paused and waited for her. When she arrived all three policemen tipped their hats to her.

"Ma'am?" Officer Hawkins added a deferential nod. He felt it was his place as the senior officer.

"These are…" Angela's mind went blank. What could she say that would assure these children were set free?

She needed a story, and a good one at that. The police were unlikely to set their prisoners free on her word alone, but they would release them into her custody if she could legitimately claim responsibility for them.

If she could claim a connection that made sense.

It was well known she didn't hire child laborers, so while the man might be one of her workers—although no job came readily to mind that would require him to get quite so dirty—that wouldn't give her any authority over the children.

She certainly couldn't claim they were visiting dignitaries. People of importance rarely rolled in the mud, which appeared to be a favorite pastime of these three.

Her family was well known in Nashville, so a family connection was certainly out.

Or was it? Family extended well beyond siblings, parents, and children. She thought of certain relatives in a nearby town who had not been to Nashville for more than a decade and came up with a plan.

"They're my cousins," she blurted, concerned that she had paused too long and made the officers suspicious. Then her innate arrogance kicked in and she realized it didn't matter if the officers were suspicious. Her family ran this town. She pointed her nose in the air and schooled her voice to its normal, haughty tones.

"My cousins." She gave a nod at each of the three prisoners. "What are you doing with my cousins?"

The sudden hauteur confused Officer Hawkins. Angela was known for being firm, but fair. Her workers liked her because she didn't put on airs, unless she had to deal with someone who had overstepped his place.

Had he done something wrong?

"They're from out of town," Angela clarified, her left eyebrow rising nearly to her hairline.

Officer Bobby was new to Nashville and had no clue who this woman was or why she was blocking their way. She dressed rich, but that didn't give her the right to interfere with police business.

Especially when she was lying. Tramps and wealth didn't mix; they came from different spheres of society. He wasn't sure why she had decided to make such an outlandish claim, but he wasn't having any of it.

Women were the strangest creatures and he had yet to meet one with an ounce of common sense. One minute they'd be giggling over puppies, and the next hysterically crying because a spider crawled across the floor.

This one had quite likely chosen these tramps as her new pet project.

No matter. He knew how to handle the situation. Back home he was known as the witty one. He knew exactly what to do to lighten the mood. And if he could prove his worth to Officer Hawkins at the same time, so much the better.

"So, missy," Officer Bobby said as he turned to Angela and mimicked the raised eyebrow. "Where are they from—Ragtown, Pennsylvania? Or maybe they're from Dirtsville, Maine."

Officer Roberts, who was far from the brightest lad on the force, snickered. He was always ready to enjoy a good joke. And Dirtsville, Maine was good joke! It sounded like the perfect place for these bums to be from.

Mid-snicker Officer Roberts caught sight of Officer Hawkins's face and his smile dropped away. That shocked look couldn't be good.

That snarky comment by Officer Bobby was the best thing that could have happened for the time travelers. Because Angela might have changed her mind about helping such a ragtag band of ruffians. But she had been insulted, and by a lowly police rookie, no less.

"Not that it's any of your concern"—Angela, who was half a foot shorter than the rookie somehow managed to look down her nose at him—"but they were viewing our farms."

Without another word Angela pointed to a spot by her side. Officer Hawkins understood the implied order and immediately brought Philip to her and released the prisoner's arms. Then he motioned for the other two officers to follow suit.

When Becca and Maddie were safely by their "cousin's" side, the officers moved away a respectful distance. Able to move freely at last, the former prisoners spent several moments stretching arms and rubbing sore shoulders.

"Who is she?" Officer Bobby whispered to Officer Hawkins.

"She belongs to one of the oldest and wealthiest families in Nashville." Officer Hawkins kept his voice so low Officer Bobby had to struggle to hear. "Don't mess with her, or her family. Not if you want to stay in the force, that is."

Then Officer Hawkins pasted a smile on his face and turned to Angela.

"Have a good day, ma'am," he said loudly as he tipped his hat.

The other two policemen followed his lead with matching hat-tips.

But they didn't move away. They stood there, silently, watching the supposed family group. What they expected to see was unclear.

"Run along, now. We don't need you anymore." Angela had had enough of the police for one day and shooed them away like they were naughty children caught in a bout of mischief.

His face red with embarrassment, Officer Hawkins led the officers away. Angela's family had too much wealth and power in Nashville to risk making her uncomfortable.

When the policemen had moved safely out of earshot Angela turned to Philip.

"You're a mess," she stated flatly.

Not exactly what Philip expected to hear. Not after the flirty looks he and Angela had exchanged. At least, he hoped they were flirty.

Angela had no time for flirting. She was known for doing the right thing at the right time. And right now, these people—who she had just claimed as cousins—needed to look more human and less like dirt statues.

"We need…" Philip paused as he pointed to

the capitol building.

"What you need is to clean up. You'll never get anywhere looking like that."

Philip, Maddie, and Becca exchanged a look, which Angela correctly interpreted meant that a time issue was at hand.

"My house is close," she assured them. "You can clean up there. The voting won't start for a while yet. These things take time."

The youngest boy gave a nod to the older boy, who turned to the man and gave a nod. The man turned to Angela and passed the nod along to her.

"Lead the way," the man said.

"What should I call you?" Angela asked. "I should know the names of my cousins."

She wasn't sure what to think about the whole nod business—it almost seemed like one of the youngsters was in charge. But there was no need to think about that now. She needed to get these three out of here.

"Philip."

"And the boys?"

"Umm, these…umm, boys…they're called Bec and Mad."

Angela heard the hesitation in his voice and wondered about it. Could it be that this man, Philip, was unsure if she was trustworthy?

He was a stranger to these parts. He most likely had not heard of her and her family. He had hesitated at the names of the boys because he wanted to protect them.

It was quite noble, really. One of those rare cases where a man's looks were matched by his actions.

Angela gave a quick nod and turned to lead the trio through the crowd. Usually navigating a group through a sea of humanity was a difficult task. Someone inevitably stepped between the leader and her followers, or the followers swerved left when they should have swerved right, and before anyone knew what had happened the entire group was adrift and lost.

But Angela wasn't worried. The crowd had thinned significantly as hungry protestors headed home to refill their bellies. Those who had chosen to stay behind were busy with picnic lunches.

The churning sea of humanity had calmed to a tidal pool.

Everything would have been fine if a wave of new protestors, all of them sporting red roses, hadn't swooshed in and flooded the area. In the blink of an eye, Philip and "the boys" were swamped by a sea of red and Angela was nowhere in sight.

Philip stood his ground and tried to keep tabs on Becca and Maddie as they were jostled about by the crowd. He saw the moment a particularly rough man with a robust red rose in his buttonhole spotted Maddie's yellow scarf.

Philip groaned as he realized the man probably mistook the scarf for a symbol of the opposition. His fear was confirmed when the rough man reached down, grabbed Maddie by the collar, and lifted her off the ground.

"What have we here?" the man, known as Burt, growled as he lifted the wriggling child in the air.

Maddie kicked and struggled as she grasped the handkerchief around her neck. The handkerchief was being used to swing her in the air like a noose and was effectively cutting off her windpipe. Then her kicks became weak and pitiful as she was forced to turn her focus on not passing out.

Philip and Becca were horrified by the sight of Maddie dangling helplessly in the air. They tried to rush to her aid but were stopped by a blockade of men obviously intent on mischief. Several of the men grabbed hold of the would-be rescuers.

"This little fella's a traitor to his kind," Burt bellowed. "Thinks womenfolk—"

Before Burt could inform the mob around him what the little fella thought about womenfolk, Angela shoved her way into the center of the group. And since she was practically royalty in Nashville, the men stepped back to give her room.

"Burt, put down the child." Angela's voice rang out clear and loud.

Burt hesitated. It made him feel powerful to hold this traitor in the air like this. He liked feeling powerful. He didn't want to stop, it felt good.

And why should he stop! No woman was going to tell him—

"There's a line of men waiting to take your job at the factory," Angela reminded Burt when she saw his chin tighten mutinously.

Burt may have decided to listen to Angela, but Becca was too quick for him. She broke free from her captors and sent a swift, hard kick to Burt's shin. Burt dropped Maddie like a hot potato and she plopped to the ground in a heap.

"Hey!" Burt yelled as he grabbed his aching leg. "No cause for violence."

Becca ignored Burt and rushed to Maddie's

side to rip the scarf from around her sister's throat. Maddie's breathing was ragged and harsh, and it was only after several hacking coughs that the child felt strong enough to be helped to her feet.

When Maddie was on her feet Becca led her to Angela's side.

"These people are with me," Angela said firmly. She put an arm across Maddie's shoulder and guided her away.

Most of the men in the group worked for Angela and her family. As she moved forward the crowd split to form an easy pathway. Becca followed close behind.

Philip jerked his arms free of his captors, gave them a dirty look, then followed his new benefactor.

The crowd closed in behind them and they were swallowed by a sea of red roses.

CHAPTER 18

PHILIP HAD EXPECTED ANGELA to live in a nice house. Her clothing and the attitude of the police officers pointed to the woman having money. But the ritzy street she led them to far outpaced any of his expectations.

These weren't houses, they were mansions. Complete with a plethora of servants—gardeners, maids, butlers, chauffeurs, etc.—who all gave the muddy trio a wide berth and stared at them as if they were lepers.

Or maybe those looks were more glare than a stare. A couple of them seemed ready to toss them in the trash, until they saw Angela.

For her part, Angela never noticed the effect her guests had on the neighborhood servants. She led them, oblivious to onlookers, to the biggest, richest, best-kept mansion on the block.

Mansion didn't do it justice, really. It was more a palace. It was that big and impressive.

As she turned to walk up the front pathway Philip stopped her.

"You live...here?"

"My entire life." Angela's smile was warm with nostalgia as visions of a happy childhood flashed in her head. "Great little house for kids. Plenty of nooks and crannies to play hide-and-seek."

Philip had to clamp down hard on his tongue to keep back the comment sitting on the end of it. This "little house" was the biggest mansion he'd ever seen. He waited until Angela had turned back to look at her house, then he made a what-do-you-think look at Maddie and Becca.

In perfect synchronization the girls responded with this-is-crazy faces and a shrug.

How did they do that? Philip wondered. He'd never seen them practicing.

Maybe it was part of that sister thing they had talked about. He'd never get used to it, no matter how many times he saw the phenomenon.

Philip decided that the shrug meant they were okay with going to Angela's house, so he shrugged in return and followed Angela up the pathway.

They had made it all the way to the front door when, her hand on the knob, Angela paused to look back at her guests. She blinked a several times in shock. She had somehow forgotten the extreme level of dirt that covered every square inch of her cousins.

Only, they weren't her cousins. And her family would know that.

"Let's go around back. Easier," she suggested. She dropped her hand from the doorknob and led her new friends around the house to the back.

CHAPTER 19

QUICKER THAN THE TIME traveling sisters thought possible they had washed the grime from their persons and slipped into the loose pajamas provided for them. They had been asked to leave their filthy clothing on the bathroom floor to be cleaned, a request neither child had a problem with.

Refreshed and feeling more like themselves than they had since they said goodbye to their mother and sisters in that warehouse in Seattle, the sisters stepped out of the bathroom to find a maid waiting for them. She handed each of them a light blanket to drape over their shoulders and led them down the hall to a guest room set aside for their use.

It was just one guest room of many in the gigantic house, but oh, what a work of art! It was kid-friendly and, by far, the most gorgeous bedroom the girls had ever seen.

In the center of the large, airy room was the most beautiful four-poster bed imaginable. Across from the bed, on the outer wall, a row of open windows let in both a cooling breeze that danced the curtains in a merry jig and the warm summer sun that lit the room with gold. Every inch of that wonderful room was decorated to inspire happiness, from the light, bright color scheme to the soft texture of the wallpaper to the perfect ratio of furniture to open space.

As the maid closed the door Becca's eyes darted around the room. She was looking for a good place to sit. And though a plethora of chairs were dotted strategically along the walls, Becca decided to ignore them in favor of the soft comfort of the edge of the bed.

Maddie had no desire to sit and immediately began exploring the room. Which for Maddie, meant closing her eyes and touching everything in reach. She ran her hand along the wall and smiled at the velvety texture. She bumped her hand along the ornate edge of the dresser and grinned as the intricate design tickled her fingertips.

The tactile exploration continued until she ran into what her hands told her was a stack of books. Her eyes flew open and she quickly read the titles.

"Look! *The Time Machine*!" she said excitedly to her sister.

Becca hopped off the bed and joined her at the dresser. The book in question was third in the pile and Becca slid it out to look it over. It was dogeared and scuffed, a sure sign it had been read many times.

"Someone likes this one." She grinned. "Good taste!"

She lifted the top two books and put the book back where she'd found it. Then she joined her sister to explore every inch of the room.

It was fun for a bit, but after every surface had been touched and every drawer opened the girls were done. Even the most interesting and well-decorated of bedrooms was still only a bedroom.

Explorations complete, the sisters shrugged in perfect unison and returned to the bed to sit side by side on its edge. They weren't quite to the thumb twiddling stage, but if body language was any indication, and it was, they were most assuredly ready for something new. Anything new.

"Where's Philip?" Maddie asked.

Becca shot a searching look at her sister. Had she thawed toward Philip?

If she had asked the question aloud Maddie would have said no, and she would have been telling the truth.

Philip still held the top spot on Maddie's least favorite people list. And she was pretty sure he'd always be there. She truly could not see herself ever forgiving him. Especially since it was selfishness that had set this whole mess in motion.

Philip had wanted to change the past so he could get a job. A job!

And her dad had died.

Maddie knew that jobs were usually necessary for adults, but if Philip had simply stayed in his own time and found a way to be happy with his life, her dad would still have a life.

So no, her feelings toward Philip were as frosty as they ever were. Frankly, she couldn't care less about Philip's whereabouts.

Except she was smart enough to know, even if she wasn't ready to admit it to her sister, that they needed him to complete their mission. He was a necessary member of her timeline repairing squad.

"Probably put him in a fancy room, one not for kids." Becca scrunched up her nose to show her disdain of the type of pretentious rooms meant for adults.

Maddie nodded. To delay the wave of boredom she felt looming over her left shoulder, she twiddled her thumbs. It did no good and only brought the wave of boredom crashing down on her head.

With a sigh she threw herself back onto the bed. At least she could stare at the pristine white ceiling. If she looked hard enough, maybe she could discover a few hidden patterns.

"What do you think they did with our clothes?" Becca asked when the silence again became too burdensome.

"Burned them?" Maddie quipped.

Becca blinked several times as she thought, then she turned to her sister with a smile on her face.

"Yeah," Becca said. She jumped off the bed, grabbed her sister's hand, and pulled her upright.

"Probably thought they were infected."

Becca continued with a twinkle in her eye and playful tone of voice.

It was enough to spark Maddie's interest and she hopped off the bed.

"With poverty," Maddie added after a slight pause.

Becca looked at Maddie and grinned. This was an old game the girls had played often, usually when they were forced to wait patiently for long periods of time with nothing to occupy their hours.

The rules were simple: take some mundane happening and build it into a story. The sillier the better.

"But maybe they didn't know the clothes should be burned. Maybe—"

Becca stopped and grinned. The grin was enough for Maddie; she knew exactly what was in her sister's mind and began to speak as if she were narrating a horror movie.

"No one knew the danger they had brought into their home," Maddie began.

"Until one night—"

"Day," Maddie corrected as she motioned to the bright sunlight streaming in the window. Becca nodded her acceptance of the correction.

Becca gave a nod toward the window. "Until

the day the clothes came to life—"

"Infected clothes," Maddie interrupted. "That has to be in there."

Becca nodded as she continued in her best horror story narrator voice.

"Infected by..." Becca paused for four full seconds before she continued. "Infected by the deadly poverty disease—"

"They began to prowl," Maddie added.

Becca squinted her eyes, as if watching a creeping creature. "Creeping about, ready to pounce—"

"Searching for the next unsuspecting victim." Maddie opened her eyes wide, apparently to mimic how the infected creatures search for their victims.

"Creeping about," Becca continued, "ready to pounce—"

"You said that already," Maddie complained.

"What do you expect?" Becca shrugged, taking herself momentarily out of the story. "It's just shirts and pants. How scary can shirts and pants be?"

Always ready for any challenge, Maddie decided to show her sister exactly how scary shirts and pants could be.

"Whoooo! I'm a scary shirt!" She lifted both

her arms and held them out stiffly in front of her. Then she began walking around with equally stiff legs, zombie style. Before long both girls had forgotten all their cares and were giggling up a storm.

It was a relief to let down their guard like this. They had spent so much time lately in their boy personas. Being able to be themselves was like donning a cozy sweater on a chilly day. It felt right.

Unfortunately, they weren't quite as alone as they thought. Unknown to either girl, Jane, Angela's twelve-year-old daughter, had cracked open the door and was watching her two young guests at play.

"Scary pants!" Maddie yelled as she pulled herself together after a particularly virulent bout of giggles and resumed her zombie-ish walk. "Watch out! They might—"

But then she realized she was stuck. She tilted her head to the side as she thought through her next move.

"What would scary pants do?" she asked when nothing came to mind.

"I don't know." Becca made a funny face as she tried to project herself into a pair of scary pants. "Maybe make a person walk funny?"

Maddie walked about the room, contorting

her legs in strange ways as she pretended she was wearing pants that fought her every step.

Becca, never one to stand on the sideline, climbed on the bed.

"And scary pants wouldn't let you do this," she said as she began to jump on the springy surface.

Maddie fought the imaginary scary pants she was wearing over to the bed, then pretended to try to climb up, but her scary pants wouldn't let her.

"No! Help!" she yelled. "The scary pants have got me. I can't bend my knees! Help!"

"Sister rescue!" Becca yelled. She grabbed Maddie by her underarms and pulled her up on the bed. Once she got her onto the bed it took a little effort to help the younger girl stand. Her sister was wearing zombie pants, after all, and couldn't bend her legs. But Becca managed it somehow and soon Maddie was jumping away on the bed. She even remembered to keep her legs awkwardly straight most of the time.

The two youngsters continued to joke and giggle, having a good old time.

Jane had seen enough. She quietly retracted her head and gently closed the door.

"Applesauce," she muttered as she blew a twig of her kinky-curly red hair back from her face. Her hair was always getting in the way, which was the only reason she agreed to keep it in braids, like her mother wanted. "If those two are boys I'll eat Aunt Sara's hat!"

The young girl stood in the hallway for several minutes as she thought through what she had seen. Each new idea brought a new expression which made her many freckles dance merrily on her face.

"Sister rescue, not brother rescue. Hmph!"

Jane stiffened her chin and it led the way as she marched down the hall to the storeroom where clothing for the poor was stored. She had been given the job of picking out suitable clothing for those two fakers. No one had said whose definition of suitable had to be used.

"They fooled Mother...for now...but they don't fool me! Bet I can make them spill the beans. They can't keep secrets from me!"

She quickly made her choices and marched back down to the hall to the guest bedroom. Jane wanted to break in and catch the girls jumping on the bed. She was sure it would embarrass them, and she wanted them to be embarrassed. It would be their punishment for lying to her mother.

But when Jane reached the door she paused, her hand on the doorknob. Her mother had always taught her that it was of the utmost importance to treat guests with respect. A Southern lady always made her guests comfortable. Anything less was rude, and rude was not done.

With a sigh Jane removed her hand from the knob and grudgingly knocked. As loud as she could. Then she took a step back and did something that was very hard for her: She waited patiently.

Inside the room that loud knock shocked the sisters into a frenzied moment of panic. They had been caught up in play and had pushed reality so far into the background that they might as well have been startled awake from a dream.

Maddie jumped to the edge of the bed and tried to climb down but forgot that her legs could bend. Becca grabbed her arm just in time, and hand-in-hand the sisters scrambled off the bed.

But when they tried to slide into their boyish personas they got a shock. They somehow couldn't remember how to do it.

Maddie calmly continued to try out different poses she considered boyish. She figured one of them would spark a memory that would let her slide back into the mindset she'd lived for the past few weeks.

But Becca had enjoyed being herself a little too much. Tears welled in her eyes and she threw herself onto her arms across the bed. Maddie immediately stopped the poses and went to her sister to put a sympathetic hand on her shoulder.

"Becca?" Maddie asked.

"I'm tired of being a boy." Becca's face was crammed in her arms, so her voice was muffled. "I don't want to pretend anymore."

"I know." Maddie patted Becca's back softly. "But you gotta."

"Why have I gotta?" The heat of anger dried Becca's tears in an instant. She slid to her feet and glared at her sister. "Why can't I act like a girl?"

"It's just pretend, Becca." Maddie used the same soft, cajoling voice she usually reserved for her four-year-old sister. She wasn't sure why Becca was acting like a four-year-old, but she recognized the tone and knew what to do. "Like zombie pants."

"I know that." Becca stomped her foot in frustration, then realized what she had just done. She pulled herself together and tried to explain her point. "But—"

A second loud knock at the door froze both

girls. Their hearts plummeted to the floor as the door slowly opened. They weren't ready. Not nearly ready. Yet they somehow both managed to slide back into their boy personas without another hitch.

When Jane, a girl of their same age, walked in they breathed a sigh of relief. She had an unlit pipe in her mouth and was balancing a large stack of clothing in front of her face. Without a word she quickly crossed the room and set the pile of clothing on the bed.

Jane took a quick glance at the two supposed boys and nodded to herself. There was no doubt they were sisters. She chose a clean pair of trousers from the pile and handed them to the older sister.

"Thanks," the girl said as she looked over the pants. They seemed to be about the right size, but most importantly, they were clean. Becca liked the thought of wearing clean clothes again. She turned to the newcomer. "You are...?"

"Jane. My mom brought you here."

"Nice to meet you, Jane."

Becca held out her hand as a gesture of goodwill. Jane clamped down hard on the stem of the pipe with her teeth as she stared at the hand for several seconds. Then she seemed to come to some sort of decision because she shook the extended hand, turned to Maddie, and repeated the handshake.

"You two have very gentlemanly manners," Jane commended her guests as she handed Maddie a clean pair of pants and a shirt. "Where're you from?"

"West Coast," Becca quickly answered.

"Saw your clothes." Jane wrinkled her nose. "How'd you get here? Through a pig sty?"

Becca's chin jutted out, which Maddie knew meant she was offended. Before Becca said anything she might regret, Maddie stepped in.

"Rode the rails," the younger girl blurted, pride the uppermost emotion in her voice.

"You did what?" Jane asked, surprised by the answer.

"You know," Becca explained, in full control again. "It's when you hop a freight train. It takes a lot of bravery to travel that way."

"Bravery." Jane shook her head and snorted. "You're just cheap!"

Becca and Maddie exchanged confused looks. Becca opened her mouth to speak and Maddie shook her head, but the older girl ignored her.

"Why are you calling us cheap?" Becca asked.

"What else could you be? People don't ride in the pig car of trains for the fun of it."

"We didn't ride with pigs!" Becca yelled. She was getting very frustrated with this girl.

"You must have, 'cause your clothes looked, and smelled, like you rolled in a pig sty!" Jane yelled back.

"There were no pigs!" Becca was losing her cool, so Maddie stepped in.

"The mud was from getting off the train," Maddie explained. "I lost my balance and fell. Philip and...Beck...had to jump after me to save me. No one expected the giant puddle of mud."

Jane took a step back as she looked over the two girls. They were smaller than she was, and certainly didn't look any stronger. Why did they get to have adventures while she was stuck at home studying with tutors?

She wanted adventures, had for several years. Desperately. Her teeth clamped down on the pipe as she thought about all the adventure books she'd read.

At first, she'd stuck to books with girl heroes. Until she discovered that authors rarely wrote girl heroes, and when they did it was usually about the girl's struggle to get the attention of a man she wanted to marry.

Boring, boring, boring!

So, she became a lot less picky and read every adventure book she could find. She solved the problem of "being" the hero by pretending she dressed as a boy so no one would stop her having adventures.

One of the most exciting books she'd read was about a boy who rode the rails with a group of hobos. He went all over the country, met a lot of interesting people, and survived danger after danger. He even thwarted a bank robbery!

She'd daydreamed herself in the role many times. She even tried on a pair of pants from the homeless pile so she would know what wearing pants felt like. But she knew she'd never get the chance to experience a true adventure, even dressed as a boy. Her mother would never, *ever*, allow such a thing.

Jane glared at Maddie's short hair and fumed. This girl had done exactly what Jane had dreamed of doing: She had disguised herself as a boy and gone adventuring.

It wasn't fair!

She speared Maddie with the most intense glare she could muster, full of pent-up frustration and displeasure, expecting the girl to melt into a puddle of fear at her feet.

There was no melting, or fear. Maddie had

three sisters, and although they loved each other and usually got along, they weren't always nice to each other. She had had more fear-inducing looks thrown her way than Jane could ever imagine. She'd grown a thick, protective layer of armor eons ago.

"Applesauce," Jane muttered. She only used her favorite expletive when her mother wasn't around. Her mother didn't approve of her using vulgar words. She said they were unladylike and low class.

No one ever complained about Uncle James's bad language. But then again, he was a man. Men didn't have to worry about being ladylike.

"Applesauce!" Jane said again, only this time louder. Then she forgot all about the need to be ladylike and allowed her face to contort in frustration as she yelled, "Why. Are. You. Here?"

Becca and Maddie exchanged a look and Jane's face relaxed into a satisfied smile. She had seen that look before, many times. It always appeared right before she got what she wanted, which in this case was answers.

She loved it that people feared redheads.

By nature, she was an easygoing person, willing to go along with the wishes of others, as long as it didn't cause her too much distress.

But everybody has a bad day once in a while. One stormy day when she was four, a new nurse neglected to give her a snack, which made her cranky. Then the nurse told her she needed a nap, but Jane felt she was too old for a nap.

When a couple of maids came to see what all the ruckus was about, Jane overheard the nurse explain that redheads had explosive tempers. That was just the way it was.

She may have only been four, but even a four-year-old can recognize an opportunity when it falls in her lap. If no one wanted to risk a tantrum, she could use that to her advantage. Talk about a life-changing revelation!

Jane crossed her arms and tapped her left foot as she waited. It was a pose that had often brought about good results.

Since Jane had already failed in her stare-down with the younger girl, she focused her glare on the older girl. Yet, the older girl still didn't start talking. She didn't so much as look at Jane. Neither girl was looking at Jane.

Instead, the older girl slowly and methodically unfolded the clothes and laid them out on the bed as the younger girl watched. When both the pants and the shirt were neatly laid out, the girl picked up the pants and measured them against her legs.

"These should fit," she said. "Mind leaving, so we can change?"

Jane raised her brows in shock, then scowled. But these expressions were lost on the two girls, who still refused to look her way.

Quite often Jane's expressions of anger were an act, a ruse to get her way.

But Jane was angry now. She couldn't believe these two had no intention of telling her anything! They honestly thought it was a good idea to leave her out, in her own house!

"Please," the older girl asked. No, asked was the wrong word because there was no real question. It was a command.

Suddenly, Jane understood. These two pretenders didn't know that she knew that they were pretenders. They still thought she thought they were boys.

Instead of doing the expected, which was to be a good little girl and follow the orders of the males of her species, Jane pasted a saccharine smile on her face and turned to the younger of the two.

"How about yours?" she asked sweetly. "Think they'll fit?"

Maddie, suspicious of that fake-sweet smile,

unfolded the pants she had been given and held them up. They were so tiny they only *might* fit a five-year-old and were probably intended for a toddler.

"Hey!" she complained. Did this redhead honestly think Maddie could fit into baby pants, or was this some sort of game she was playing?

Jane grabbed a piece of clothing from the pile she had brought to the room and pitched it at Maddie with an arm that would impress any baseball coach. Maddie barely managed to catch it before it slapped her in the face.

"Maybe you'd rather get gussied up," the redhead yelled, her chin jutting out bulldog style.

The source of Jane's anger was jealousy, pure and simple. Her main desire in life was to have an adventure, any adventure, but had always been told adventures were for boys. Girls were expected to stay home, have babies, and keep the home fires burning. It was the way things were, the way they had always been, the way they needed to be.

Jane had bemoaned her fate, that by a fluke of nature she'd been born into a dress instead of pants and therefore had a whole world of opportunities denied to her.

But she had watched her mother run the family business and knew that it was possible to step outside the gender rules set by society. If a girl had a family that backed her up.

Only…although Jane's family would happily support her if she wanted to run a business, they drew the line at adventuring. That would be carrying things too far.

She'd eventually come to terms with her fate and had settled on another plan. She would choose an adventurer as a husband. If she couldn't go on adventures, she could at least live vicariously, through her husband. It wasn't quite the same thing, but it was as close as she was likely to get.

Of course, she might be lucky enough to find a husband who allowed her to tag along with him on one or two adventures. The less dangerous ones. But even that opportunity would go away as soon as she had a baby.

Jane looked again at these two girls pretending to be boys and nearly growled. How dare they do what she'd never had the nerve to do!

Years of pent-up frustration ripped off the scab that had formed on Jane's wounded ambition and oozed to the surface. It hurt dreadfully. And like every other creature that's in pain, Jane was ready to lash out.

Maddie, who saw the pain in Jane's eyes but didn't understand why it was there, cautiously unfolded the piece of clothing Jane had thrown at her. When she held it up the color drained from her face. It was a dress. What did this girl know?

"You too." Jane grabbed another dress from the pile to hurl it at Becca. "Want some glad rags for yourself?"

But Becca wasn't having any of it and simply let the dress fall to the floor.

"What would I want with that?" Becca asked in a firm, steady voice. She was the oldest of four and recognized the deep anger of jealousy when she saw it. She knew she had to keep her cool, because jealousy sometimes made people unpredictable, and downright mean. "That's for girls, and we're not—"

"Don't take me for a flat tire," Jane snarled. "You're girls, both of you."

Becca's face slipped with that comment and a twinge of panic showed.

"No." Maddie stepped in to give sisterly support. Or maybe it was brotherly support, since she was supposed to be a boy. "We're—"

"Pretending," Jane stated flatly, her lip curled in disgust. "To be boys. Yeah, I know."

She gave Becca and Maddie the once-over and her lip curled so much Maddie checked behind her ear to make sure she had washed everything away.

"Think I'm a dingbat?" she asked, then she snorted. "I knew you were dames the moment I saw you."

Becca had had enough. She exchanged a quick but silent communication with her sister, then nodded. Both girls relaxed out of their boy stances. It was a subtle difference, but noticeable.

"No one else did." Becca shrugged. She stretched her arms over her head and yawned happily. It was much more relaxing to be herself.

"People see what they expect to see." Jane nodded her understanding. "I mean, really, what kind of dame rides in freight cars? I mean—"

Jane had known that these girls had dressed as boys to go adventuring and it had angered her. But she shouldn't be angry. She should be taking notes.

She chewed on the end of pipe for several seconds before she said pointedly, "Girls don't do things like that."

"Exactly." Maddie lifted her eyebrows,

hoping Jane would get the message.

Jane did. She dug a pair of pants from the pile of clothes.

"Here," Jane said as she handed the pants to Maddie. All trace of anger had disappeared. "These should do."

"Are you going to tell?" Maddie asked.

"Depends."

"On what?"

"No jiggery-pokery," Jane warned. "Tell me the truth. What are you doing here?"

Becca and Maddie did another one of their silent communications that a child with no siblings could never understand. With a nod, Maddie ran to the dresser, grabbed *The Time Machine*, and ran to stand in front of Jane.

"Ever read this?" Maddie shoved the book into Jane's hands.

"Of course." Jane lovingly ran her fingers over the cover before holding it close. "It's my favorite book."

"Good." Becca pointed to a clear space on the floor. "Have a seat. This might take a while."

The three girls sat on the floor in what they meant to be a unifying circle but was really a triangle since there were three of them. Becca gently took the book from Jane and held it up.

"Time machines," she began, "are real—"

"And so is time travel," Maddie interrupted. "We—"

Jane leaned in eagerly as Becca and Maddie told their story. The two sisters left out very little. They told her about their family's ability to easily travel through time. That in the original timeline their adult selves had invented time travel, but that they didn't really know much about that since they hadn't done it yet.

Then they told her that someone from the future—they kept Philip's name out of it—had messed up. That there were now problems with the timeline that had made the future world nearly unrecognizable.

They told her about their two younger sisters and mother waiting for them at the warehouse. And about their adventures in the future, which had led them here, to the past.

There was a long pause before they finally told her about their dad. They saved that story for last because they weren't sure if they could get all the words out. Tears flowed freely down their cheeks as they described him to Jane, and she didn't have to use any imagination to see that the girls truly loved and missed their father.

When the girls had finished speaking, Jane

sat back.

"I liked it," Jane sighed, thoroughly satisfied with the story.

Becca and Maddie wiped away the tears and watery smiles grew on their faces.

"So, you'll help us?" Becca asked. She grabbed two of the extra shirts from the pile and used one to dry her face. The other she tossed to her sister.

"I will." Jane nodded. "On one condition."

"What's that?" Maddie asked. She blew her nose into the shirt she'd just used to dry her face, which made Becca scowl.

"That you tell me what you're really up to." Jane smirked. "No gas this time. None of that H.G. Wells nonsense."

"Nonsense!" Maddie was insulted. "We spilled our guts to you, and you—"

Becca, who had been studying Jane, put a hand on Maddie's arm to shut her up. After a quick look at her sister, Maddie clamped her mouth closed.

"What makes you think we're not telling the truth?" Becca asked curiously.

"I told you I'm no flat tire!" Jane scoffed. "There's no such thing as time travel. Everybody knows that."

Jane picked up *The Time Machine* book and

waved it around.

"Makes a good story, though." Jane nodded happily. "And I liked the story you made up, too. Maybe even better."

Becca, who realized their story was a bit much for a 1920 brain to comprehend, nodded her understanding, then pierced her sister with a go-along-with-what-I-say look.

"You got us." Becca shrugged. "We made it all up."

Maddie gave a barely perceptible nod and Becca relaxed. Rarely did their silent communication fail to work properly, but it had been known to happen.

"We're here for the ratification," Becca explained. Which was the truth.

"It's time women got the right to vote," Maddie added. Becca nodded her approval.

"That's it? It's about the vote?" Jane studied the two girls who, based on their own admission, had spent the last week masquerading as boys. It could not have been easy and would have gotten them into a lot of trouble if they had been caught.

"It's as simple as that," Becca said, and her voice held a ring of truth that was undeniable.

It was as simple as that. If the girls didn't make sure the Nineteenth Amendment was ratified, women wouldn't get the right to vote, the timeline would remain changed, and her dad would die. Everything hinged on the ratification passing.

At the thought of her dad Becca felt a new wave of tears forming, but she pushed them away. The time for tears was over. She had a job to do.

"In that case, I'll help." Jane gave a firm nod of her head. "I think women should be allowed to vote, too."

Maddie's forehead crinkled in worry.

"But your mother—"

"Is against. I know."

Jane watched as Becca and Maddie exchanged another silent look, this one of concern.

"We're not the first mother and daughter to disagree, you know." Jane shrugged. She rarely went against her mother's wishes, but she felt strongly about this cause.

"Oh, we know!" Becca's eyes widened as she remembered the times she had disagreed with her mother. It, also, had not happened often. But Becca was her own person, and individuals will have disagreements from time to time. Even parents and their children.

"What are your plans?" Jane asked. "How

can I help?"

Eyes gleaming with excitement, the three girls leaned in together to talk.

CHAPTER 20

HALF AN HOUR LATER—after the three girls were done with their plotting and planning—the two sisters got dressed and headed downstairs in the guise of two spiffy boys ready to take on the world.

They found Philip waiting for them at the bottom of the grand stairway.

Philip certainly seemed to be enjoying his new duds.

"This is more like it!" Philip ran his hand across the smooth surface of his coat and smiled. "Angela actually apologized for giving it to me to wear. Said it was silk, and that it was the only suit she could find in my size."

As Philip lifted his arm, he noticed a piece of lint on his sleeve. With more caution than was warranted, he carefully brushed it away. Then he scanned the rest of the arm, ready to do battle with any extraneous material he might find.

Becca and Maddie giggled at his antics. Philip had never shown signs of vanity before. As a matter of fact, he'd worked hard to hide his good looks. This was new, and somewhat interesting.

"Angela said it's made by worms." Philip had finished with one arm and moved on to the other. "No such thing exists in my time. I mean, we have beautiful fabric, but it was formulated in a test tube and structured by a machine. How can a worm do this?"

Becca and Maddie exchanged a glance and giggled. Now they understood. Philip wasn't vain, he was a scientist. And scientists were fascinated by what they don't understand.

"I'm pretty sure the worm had help," Becca reminded Philip when he showed no sign of losing interest in the worm-created fabric.

"Worms with sewing machines," Maddie joked. "That would be something to see!"

But Philip ignored what the girls were saying because he didn't realize it was their way of steering him back to the task at hand. He knew they hadn't yet forgiven him for the part he played in breaking the timeline. He figured they were trying to give him another dig.

He again ran his hands down the front of the jacket and when they reached the bottom, tugged. He was impressed with the fabric. Smooth and strong, which allowed every segment of the suit to interact with every other segment perfectly. He straightened his cuffs and double-checked that the buttons of the jacket were aligned.

After he also straightened his collar, he looked around for a mirror. But there wasn't one available. His hand fell to his tie and he frowned. He was enough of a perfectionist to want this work of art to be as flawless as he could possibly make it.

"Is it straight?" Philip asked as he twiddled with the tie.

"Perfectly," Becca assured him. "You look great, Philip, now let's go."

"But I want to see—"

"Don't you think that's enough time spent on worm spit?" Maddie asked when Philip's fascination continued on well after Maddie thought it should end.

"Worm spit?" Philip's hands fell away from the smooth material.

"We'll find you a book later that explains how it's made," Maddie promised.

"But for now, there's a vote to change," Becca reminded him.

"And our Dad to save," Maddie added.

"And—"

But the rest of the comment remained unsaid as a loud burst of laughter erupted from a nearby room, startling the three. The laughter consisted of both men's and women's voices, and if loudness was an accurate gauge, the group was having a grand time.

"Let's just go." Becca scowled. Adults laughing had always made her uncomfortable. It stemmed from a fear that she was the source of their humor. They were laughing at her.

Becca had overcome the fear a few years ago, but she shivered anyway as she stepped toward the front door. She wanted to escape that irritating noise as fast as she could. She would have been out the door in a flash if Philip hadn't grabbed her arm. Becca turned the full brunt of her glare on him, but he simply motioned for her to be quiet.

The laughter in the other room died away and a man's voice could be plainly heard.

"So, I put it in my pocket and sent the boy away." The man's words were followed by more laughter.

Maddie took one look at Philip's face and

elbowed Becca in the ribs. Not only was Philip not laughing, but he was downright scowling. Philip didn't show his anger often and this was an extreme case of it.

"Can't be," Philip growled, as his brows formed a veritable storm cloud on his forehead.

"What?" Becca wondered what was wrong with the man. His face was puckered up like he'd just bit into a bitter lemon.

Philip pointed toward the closed double door and tried to talk, but he was so angry that the words got stuck in his throat. So, he mouthed the words *Mr. Selfish*, instead.

The girls got it instantly and their eyes grew round. Philip's anger bubbled over and he took a step toward the double doors, and it was Becca's turn to snake out a hand and grab his arm. He turned toward her, but his eyes didn't see her. In his mind he was already in the other room teaching Mr. Selfish that being selfish didn't pay.

"Philip," Becca whispered, hoping to get through to the man. "He might still have the letter."

Maddie nodded her head wildly in agreement, but Philip couldn't see her through the red haze of hate that had clouded his brain.

He was no longer thinking logically.

"Philip," Becca pleaded. "Come out of it!" She tugged on his sleeve several times, but the only response was a low, deep growl. The type that would make a person run out of the woods screaming if they heard it while out on a walk.

Becca threw a pleading glance to her sister and the younger girl jumped into action. She balled up her fist, pulled it back, and punched Philip in the arm with everything she had.

"Ouch!" Philip whispered.

Both girls breathed a sigh of relief. Philip's eyes were clear and focused once again. He was back.

"Why did you punch me?" Philip wanted to know.

"You were about to pummel Mr. Selfish," Maddie told him.

"It would have ruined any chance to fix the timeline," Becca explained.

"And besides," Maddie added, "you were being weird."

Philip blinked several times at that, then nodded.

"Are you normal now?" Becca asked.

"I am."

"You're not going to go all animal-man again, are you?" This was from Maddie, who still had her fist clenched and ready to strike.

"Animal-man?"

"You were growling, Philip. Growling!"

"I promise." Philip had the good grace to look ashamed of his loss of control.

Maddie took a step toward Philip, struck a superman pose, and her chin became steel as she pinned him with her laser eyes.

"If you do, I'm ready." Maddie punched her fist into the palm of her hand in the accepted tough guy style.

Philip, once again in full control of his emotions, still had to struggle to tamp down the grin that tried to sprout on his face. But he managed to nod solemnly instead.

"Shall we?" Becca pointed to the double door and raised a brow.

These three were united by their disgust of the selfish man who was willing to ruin countless lives for his own gain, a man Philip was sure was in that room. No one needed to ask twice. As one they tiptoed to the door and quietly slid it open.

The room on the other side of those double doors could easily be labeled a paradise by any eavesdropper worth their salt. Not a single seat faced the door.

But these eavesdroppers were newbies, so

their first thought was that it was a strange way to arrange a room. Until they realized the layout, which was a U-shape plethora of sofas and chairs, was because of a large, ornate fireplace.

It was a beautiful fireplace. The ideal focal point for a room meant for entertaining.

To create a perfect ambience the curtains were drawn to keep out the hot August sun, and a fire had been lit in that lovely fireplace. Since heat from the fire might be a problem, several overhead fans quietly whipped the air about and kept the area fresh. The result was a room that was merry, yet cozy.

The result was also a great place for those who wanted to do a little spying. All the eavesdroppers had to do was stand just on the other side of the threshold and no one could see them. If they remained quiet, they could open the door wide and watch without worrying they'd disturb the occupants of the room.

Maddie looked with interest at the room and its occupants. Rose, the youngest woman in the room, was practically invisible in a deep chair on the far side of the room. What made her invisible was not so much the deepness of her chair but the fact that Charles, her husband, sat on its arm. He effectively blocked all the light heading her way and placed her firmly in his shadow.

Angela sat on the couch with her siblings, Sara and James, their backs to the door. They were listening to a man who stood in front of a chair to the left with a letter in his hand.

It was Douglas Whitfield, AKA Mr. Selfish. Philip's wild side reasserted itself for a moment as a low growl rumbled from his nose. But Becca gave him a sharp elbow to the ribs, which brought him back to his senses.

"She even has a line about taking the rat out of ratification," Douglas said with a guffaw, which was mirrored by laughter from his audience.

"Surely a letter like that would make no difference," Angela said as the laughter died away.

"Not now!" Douglas jovially ripped the letter in half and tossed it over his shoulder dismissively. It floated slowly to the floor behind him.

He had tossed it out of his sight, but directly into Maddie's. She stared at the discarded pieces of the letter for several seconds—the very things they needed to fix the timeline—before she turned excited eyes first to her sister, then to Philip. Becca knew her well enough that she should have been able to guess what the girl was about to do, but before either of them could blink Maddie had dropped to her hands and knees and crossed the threshold.

"If he never sees it," Douglas continued, "it certainly will have no chance to change his mind. Best solution."

Maddie crawled to the back of the couch and watched for her chance to grab the letter pieces, unseen. But everyone's focus was still on Douglas. She would have to wait.

"Can't imagine a world with women voters." Angela shivered at the thought. "Horrible!"

A similar shiver made its way around the room as each occupant imagined what would happen to society if women voted.

"Poor things would need to think," Douglas said with mock sympathy. Then he dropped any semblance of sympathy and let his true feelings show through with a sneer that was downright brutal. "I've heard about women driven insane just trying to grasp logical thought."

Angela scowled at Douglas. Maddie, from behind the couch, matched her scowl exactly. The two appeared to be of one mind about

Douglas's words.

"I don't believe that for a moment." Angela raised her chin proudly.

"As well you shouldn't!" Sara grabbed Angela's hand and gave it several pats in support.

Douglas frowned, confused. These people were against ratification. The group had discussed how bad it would be for society, several times. Why would they disagree with him now?

"Women don't have the brain power to—"

Maddie, furious at Douglas's disparaging remarks about her sex, intended to jump to her feet and give him a piece of her mind. But Becca motioned for her to stay low, out of sight.

Maddie grimaced in frustration but complied. Becca was right. She needed to keep a cool head if she wanted to retrieve that letter. She'd bide her time, wait for the perfect moment, then move like the wind.

"Angela has a man's brain." James beamed proudly at his sister.

"A what?" Douglas was a shocked by such a statement coming from people who were actively working to keep women from having equal rights to men.

While the group continued their discussion about women's brains, Maddie challenged hers to figure out a way to get that letter. She flattened herself to the floor and peeked under the sofa. Past the sofa legs, past the people legs, she could make out the letter pieces near Douglas's feet. Now, if she could just figure out how to grab them without being seen.

"You know," James explained, "a brain for business. She's got better brains than me, in that noodle. She runs all our businesses."

Douglas stared at Angela, confused. She looked like a perfectly normal woman, not some oddball Brainiac who spent all her time in books. He wasn't trying to be rude but his face clearly showed how little he believed James's words.

"It's true." James shrugged and pointed to his sister. "All I do is sign where she tells me to."

"Women are not idiots, you know," Angela sniffed.

Maddie, behind the couch, motioned that she planned to rush in and get the papers.

Philip and Becca were adamant in their NO motions. They were flapping their arms about so fast it was surprising the breeze they created didn't give them away.

"Well..." James had a twinkle in his eye as he

said to his sister, "Mrs. Jones, the pharmacist's wife, is a bit—"

He gave a little whistle as he flapped his hand back and forth.

"She's just had an unfortunate upbringing," Sara argued.

Philip motioned for Maddie to stay low and go slow. Maddie nodded her understanding.

James lifted a brow to his sister, which made her sigh.

"Okay," Sara conceded, "maybe she's an idiot. But so are some men."

"Fair enough," Douglas admitted. Douglas wanted to make sure he stayed a part of the conversation and it didn't turn into a family squabble.

Maddie was willing to go low and slow, as long as she could go. She inched forward as far as she could without risking being seen. Then, slow enough that any sloth mama would be proud, she snaked a hand toward the letter pieces.

She almost had them in her grasp—she was only an inch away—when fate turned against her. Douglas, who hadn't even looked at the pieces of paper since he tossed them in the air, chose that exact moment to decide to pick them up and shove them into a side pocket of his jacket. And then he sat in the chair.

Maddie sat back in frustration. She had been so close!

"Women need protection," Angela explained. She knew not everyone would understand her position. "Most would never make it on their own."

Angela pointed toward Charles, then past him to Rose, hidden in the shadows.

"Take Rose, for example." Angela smiled at Rose. She meant for the smile to be kind, but to Rose it looked rather condescending.

Rose sank deeper into her chair. She didn't want, had never wanted, to be part of this conversation. All she wanted was to be left alone.

Maddie decided to take advantage of the attention being on the other side of the room, so she scooted quickly and quietly until she was beside Douglas's chair. From there she hoped to have a chance at that letter.

"She has no education, no skills, no way to take care of herself. Isn't that right, Rose dear?" Angela raised her brows commandingly as she waited for the response.

But Rose said not a word. Instead, she hung her head, as if in shame.

All eyes were on Rose. Now was Maddie's

chance! She slowly reached for Douglas's pocket, but just as her fingers touched the fabric Douglas unknowingly thwarted her by sitting back in his chair.

It took everything Maddie had to hold back a yell of frustration. How was she going to get that stupid letter from that stupid man when the stupid arm of the stupid chair blocked all access to that stupid pocket? Stupid, stupid, stupid!

"Poor child can barely read and certainly can't speak for herself," Angela continued. The young woman's silence proved Angela's point and spurred her on.

"Let her have money—she'd lose it...or spend it on trinkets." That brought a laugh from the men in the room.

"Make a living on her own? Not likely!" Angela shook her head sadly and sighed.

Meanwhile, Becca and Philip watched and listened from the doorway. Becca could see by Maddie's face that she was at the everything-is-stupid phase; she even kept mouthing the word *Stupid* over and over.

That wasn't good. Maddie was a bit like the Incredible Hulk. She didn't turn green or anything, but when she got really mad her brain was no longer in charge, just her emotions. She was likely to do something crazy, like yell at Mr. Selfish to give her that letter.

That would be disastrous. If Douglas Whitfield knew time travelers were on his trail, he'd be on his guard and they wouldn't be able to repair the timeline.

Becca positioned herself so that Maddie was the only one in the parlor who could see her. Then she flapped her arms around wildly. That got Maddie's attention, and she was able to mouth to her sister that she was going for Jane. Maddie nodded her understanding, and Becca dashed upstairs to retrieve their friend and co-conspirator.

"Luckily for Rose, she doesn't have to," Sara was saying in the parlor, where the discussion had continued. "She has Charles, and Charles will keep her safe."

Hearing his cue, Charles reached down and pulled Rose close. To the onlookers it was a protective gesture. But that was only because the onlookers couldn't see the whole picture.

There was a reason Rose kept to the shadows.

If she were in the light, someone might notice the badly bruised wrist that she had trouble covering with her sleeve. And Rose did not want anyone to notice.

The sleeve slipped, yet again, and she quickly fixed it. Someone might glance her way and care enough to take a closer look.

While Becca was upstairs, Philip, who had kept his position at the doorway, began to get nervous. Maddie was just a child, and an unpredictable one at that. What if she decided to take matters into her own hands and confront Douglas? That would be disastrous!

Even though he knew that Maddie blamed him for the break in the timeline, he hoped that maybe, maybe, she would listen to him. He schooled his face into the best pleading expression he could manage and motioned for Maddie to return to the safety of the hall.

He might as well have told her to stand on her head for all the good it did. Not only was Maddie inclined to disregard anything Philip wanted, but she also had a stubborn streak a mile wide. She shook her head like a dog with water in its ear and stayed put. She would not retreat, and she would get that letter.

While one little drama played out unobserved in the shadows, another continued its course in the cheerful light of the fireplace.

"My family has always kept me safe," Angela was saying, "and I know they'll keep my daughter, Jane, safe, too."

Angela turned to Sara and James, who nodded their agreement. But even though this should have reassured her, she shivered as her face darkened and she stared into the middle distance at a troubling scenario no one else could see.

"There are places…" As Angela spoke tears formed in the corners of her eyes. "Places women shouldn't have to go."

Douglas leaned forward, interested. What made Angela, obviously a strong and independent woman, want to deny that same strength and independence to other women?

"Dangerous places." It was obvious that although Angela's body was in the parlor, her mind was elsewhere. And wherever that place was, it was filled with pain and sorrow.

Philip heard none of this. He was too focused on Maddie. He anxiously watched her every move, hoping she would refrain from taking too many chances. But when he saw her crouch, ready to pounce, he knew he had to act fast.

What he needed was a distraction.

Not knowing what else to do he left his post near the doorway and slipped into a nearby room. The vase he slammed to the floor was satisfyingly loud and nearly everyone, including

Maddie, turned at the noise.

Douglas, startled into remembering why he was in that house, shoved his hand in his jacket pocket. The crinkle of that all-important letter comforted him, so he kept that hand pressed against the letter. Everything was going as planned.

"So much danger," Angela whispered.

Shocked, Douglas turned to look at Angela. Did she know his plans?

But no. She seemed to still be lost in her own troubled thoughts. He would bet she hadn't even heard that loud crash that had scared the daylights out of everyone else.

"Those maids will be in danger if they break the good china," Sara muttered.

But Angela didn't hear her sister's quip. She grabbed her brother's arm and turned to him, pain and worry transforming her face into a mask of agony.

"You'll keep Jane safe, won't you, James? Always?"

"Not to worry." James patted her hand gently. He had rarely seen Angela this distressed. "You can count on the menfolk to protect their womenfolk."

"That's right," Charles chimed in. He looked down at his wife lovingly. "My Rose is delicate.

I'd hate to see what would happen to her if she tried to be on her own."

To demonstrate his husbandly concern, Charles pulled Rose tightly to his side. Due to the shadows no one could see that his grip was so tight that under Rose's sleeve a new bruise was blooming, just as no one could see that Rose's smile covered a wince of pain.

Maddie knew her chance to snatch the letter had slid away as soon as Mr. Selfish slid his hand into his pocket to check the letter was still there. So, while everyone's attention was focused on Rose and Charles, Maddie scuttled back to the couch.

"Such a cute couple!" Sara smiled at Rose and Charles. "Rose, you really are lucky to have such a caring husband. Not all of them are, you know."

Rose forced a brighter smile onto her face while she nodded. But she said not a word. She found it was easier not to say the wrong thing if she simply kept her mouth shut.

Meanwhile, Maddie, who was frustrated at her failure, crawled from the back of the couch through the doorway and didn't stop crawling until she had found Philip.

"Where's Becca?" she whispered as she climbed to her feet and brushed off her knees.

"We've got to find a way to get that letter."

Philip pointed up the stairs. Maddie, tired of crawling about on the ground, bolted up the steps to find her sister.

In the parlor Sara continued to praise the young couple.

"Rose is precious, Charles," she reminded him. "Cherish her. Always."

"I know my responsibility, don't worry." Charles squeezed Rose's shoulder so hard Rose had to bite her lip to keep from crying out. "I'll never let her go."

Someone could have noticed Rose's pain. But no one did.

Someone could have realized that something was wrong in the relationship between Rose and Charles. That Charles's loving hugs had an overly possessive tinge to them. But no one did.

No one noticed anything.

It was understandable, really. Few people notice what goes on in the shadows, and Charles was very careful to keep Rose out of the limelight and in his shadow.

All under the guise of "protecting her."

Since her marriage to Charles, Rose had stopped being the outgoing talkative young woman she had always been and had become a shrinking violet.

And no one noticed.

But if they had, it was unlikely they would have said anything. Society dictated that what happened between married couples stayed between married couples. To intervene or ask questions was rude and uncouth.

It simply was not done.

CHAPTER 21

"SPEAKING OF RESPONSIBILITIES..."

Douglas pulled the pieces of the letter Maddie had tried so hard to get out of his pocket.

"I'd better destroy this letter before it manages to float out of my pocket and into Mr. Burn's hand." He held the pieces up in the air and flapped them about. Then he spotted the fire in the fireplace and he grinned.

"Do you mind?" he asked the siblings on the couch. He had every intention of tossing the letter in the fire no matter what the siblings said, but it tickled his funny bone to ask.

It was always funny when he tricked people into being complicit. These people were going to help him change the timeline, and they wouldn't even know it!

"Not at all," James replied. He leapt to his

feet, sauntered to the fireplace, and laid a hand on the screen. "Let me get the screen for you."

But the screen was much heavier than James expected and moving it was quite a chore. Usually a servant handled it, so he'd never before had a reason to touch the massive thing. While James struggled to move the weighty screen, Philip was nearly having an apoplexy in the hall.

Becca, Maddie, and Jane appeared at the top of the stairs and were surprised to see Philip at the bottom flapping his hands like a maniac.

"Hurry up!" Philip hissed. "He's going to burn the letter!"

Without another second's thought the three girls rushed downstairs. Maddie and Becca formed a huddle with Philip while Jane went directly to the threshold. She felt she needed to get caught up, and the best way to do that was to see for herself what was going on.

"If he burns that letter it's over. I don't think…" Philip shook his head.

"Distract him," Maddie interrupted. "Just until we can come up with a plan."

"How am I supposed to do that?"

"I don't know." Maddie shrugged. "Pretend you're besties or something."

"Besties?" This was a word Philip had never heard before and he was thoroughly confused. "What's a bestie?"

"A friend," Becca explained with a roll of her eyes. "A best friend."

"I can't do that!" Philip was horrified at the thought of pretending to be friends with a weasel like Douglas. "I can't—"

"Mother?" Jane's voice, loud and clear, was coming from the parlor. "What's going on in here?"

What Philip could or couldn't do was instantly forgotten. The trio turned stunned faces to look for Jane, and when she wasn't there, they rushed to the parlor door.

Inside the parlor, Jane's entrance had acted like a pause button, freezing everyone in place. The tableau included James holding the fireplace screen out of the way, Rose nearly invisible in the depths of her chair, and Sara, Angela, and Charles leaning forward eagerly, as if for a sporting event. Douglas, the focal point of the scene, held a ripped envelope over the fire, ready to drop it in.

"What's that?" Jane wanted to know. She was pointing to the ripped envelope in Douglas's hand.

Douglas looked at the letter. Nobody else so

much as twitched a nose hair.

"Give that to me," Jane commanded. As a daughter of the household she expected people to listen when she gave an order. While she was in her own house, at least.

Douglas, who had no intention of giving the letter to anyone, opened his fingers and dropped it into the fire. But Jane was quicker than expected, and by the time it had floated down to the flames she had crossed the room and used a poker to snatch it out.

With a glare at the man who had dared try to burn what she had asked for, she stomped on the smoldering paper to make sure each tiny flame had been extinguished. Then she picked up the two halves and looked at them.

"What do you think you're doing, little girl?" Douglas growled, and he grabbed Jane's arm. He had been so close to success that Jane's interference had short-circuited his natural cunning and sent his common sense scurrying up the chimney.

Because grabbing Jane's arm was definitely a mistake. Angela, Jane's mother, was very protective of her child. She had no intention of allowing any man—and particularly not a *stranger* who was a guest in her home—to treat her child so roughly.

"Do not touch my daughter," Angela warned, venom dripping from each word.

Douglas, reminded where and when he was, looked at his hand on Jane's arm, then around the parlor. The faces turned his way were stiff and unfriendly. He dropped Jane's arm like it burned and put his hand behind his back.

"The West Coast might be different," James added in frosty tones, "but here we don't go into people's homes and manhandle their children."

"My apologies." Douglas bowed to the siblings, then to Jane. "I just wanted my letter."

"Give him his letter, Jane." Angela's voice had that no-nonsense quality that Angela typically used for workers and rarely for her daughter.

"But Mother," Jane argued, "it isn't—"

"Jane!" Angela ordered sharply.

Jane unwillingly handed the letter to Douglas, but her sulky face let everyone know she was being forced to do it. Douglas gave a quick bow to his hosts—which gave Philip and the girls just enough time to scurry away—followed by an even quicker exit.

The awkward silence that was left at his exit weighed heavily on each person's thoughts. Angela was the first to shake it off. She looked at the expensive watch on her wrist and sighed.

"We'd better get going if we want to get to see the action," she said.

"Going to the capitol?" Jane asked.

Angela nodded.

"I'm coming too, Mother," she said boldly. "Just let me go get...the boys."

"Very well," Angela agreed. She didn't have the energy to argue with her daughter, not after the morning she'd had.

CHAPTER 22

ON THE WALK TO the capitol the group naturally broke apart into two segments. While Philip and Angela kept a steady pace toward their destination, Becca, Maddie, and Jane were distracted, and unnoticed by the adults, had lagged behind.

But it wasn't normal distractions that slowed the girls down. There was no smelling of flowers or watching of dogs. No, the girls kept at a snail's pace because, quite frankly, it's nearly impossible for two people to walk quickly with their heads glued together.

Not literally, of course. It was simply that Becca and Maddie were in the midst of an intense strategy session, which for them meant a constant stream of hissing whispers.

They were quite lucky, really, to have Jane along. They were too focused on their discussion and would have crashed, slipped, or tripped multiple times if Jane hadn't taken it upon herself to play pilot and guide. She did a great job of steering them past the many dangers found on a city sidewalk.

And as she steered, she chewed on her pipe and wondered at the girls' closeness. Two peas in a pod. That's what those two sisters were. So close they could even sometimes communicate without words. It had to be nice to be so close to another person that you sometimes thought the same thoughts.

The girls had stopped walking, so Jane allowed herself to daydream about having a sister. She was imagining what it would be like to whisper secrets to a sister while drifting off to sleep when she heard her name called. She looked up and was startled to find Becca and Maddie finished their plotting and had moved to flank her on each side.

"Your mother doesn't want women to get the right to vote," Becca said accusingly.

"I know," Jane sighed.

"Why?" Maddie wanted to know. "She's smart. She must know women can—"

"She's protecting me," Jane interrupted, peeved that she had to admit such a thing.

"From what?" Becca asked.

"Stress. Bother." Jane shrugged. "Having to take care of myself."

Becca and Maddie exchanged a look that Jane interpreted to mean they either didn't believe her or didn't understand. She gave another sigh and enlightened them.

"When the men went off to war, my mom and Aunt Sara had to run all the businesses," Jane explained. "But Aunt Sara was a bit of a Dumb Dora at it, so my mom took over."

Jane contemplated Angela, walking ahead with Philip. There was enough of a gap that she knew her mother couldn't hear what she was about to say.

"I think she liked it, until my dad was killed."

"What happened?" Maddie asked, her eyebrows drawing together in concern.

"She went all out for the war effort," Jane said. "Pushed herself, and everyone around her. She even started teaching me how to run the businesses."

"And?" Becca prodded when Jane's pause dragged out too long.

"There was an accident at one of our munitions factories." Jane closed her eyes for a second and took a deep breath before she continued. "An explosion. Nearly a hundred women were killed."

The three stood stock still as the horror of such an explosion sunk in. Jane swallowed.

"After that, my mother wasn't the same." She shook her head sadly. "She said it was her fault all those mothers and daughters were killed."

"Jane! Boys! Catch up!" Angela yelled. Jane looked toward her mother and realized she was nearly a block ahead. And based on the scowl on her face she was none too happy that she was being forced to yell. "And Jane, take that nasty pipe out of your mouth."

A gardener in a nearby yard snickered, then turned away when he caught Jane's eye. Jane and her pipe were a well-known pair in the neighborhood. Most of the servants found it amusing that a wealthy young girl would rebel in such a way, but out of respect for the family they all hid that amusement.

"Yes, Mother," Jane yelled in return after she'd sent a quick glare at the gardener's back. Then she grabbed her walking companions by the arms and led them at a faster pace.

"She hasn't let me do anything interesting since," Jane complained to Becca and Maddie. "But maybe if she knew you were girls..."

Jane's voice trailed off and her feet slowed as her brain focused on a new thought. Then, she obviously had come to some sort of decision because her eyes lit up and a smile sprouted across her face.

"I'd better put this away first," she muttered as she took the pipe out of her mouth and slid it into her pocket. Then without any further warning she raced toward her mother.

The two sisters locked eyes and panicked.

"No, Jane," Becca yelled. "Don't tell her!"

Becca and Maddie tried to catch up with Jane to talk sense into the girl, but she had too much of a head start. The redhead reached Angela and Philip well ahead of "the boys."

"Don't tell me what?" Angela wanted to know.

"They're girls, Mother! They're not boys. They're girls, like me!" Jane blurted in excitement.

"Jane…" Angela shook her head as she rolled her eyes. She might need to restrict Jane's reading. The girl was entirely too prone to fly off on one of these flights of fancy. "How many times have I told you there's a time and place for imagination. This isn't it."

"No, Mother!" Jane continued, and Angela sighed as she noticed that Jane showed no sign of quitting this little game she'd decided to play. "They're here to make sure women get the right to vote—"

"Jane, hush." Angela looked around to see if any of the neighbors had noticed Jane's outlandish ravings. Her family had a reputation to uphold, and Jane was on the border of damaging it badly. It could be that Angela had been too lenient with the girl.

"Applesauce!" Jane stomped her foot in frustration.

"Language, Jane. A lady always uses proper language." Angela was shocked at her daughter. Now she was certain she'd been too lenient.

"Mother, I'm not making this up." Jane stomped her foot a second time. "Ask them! They're dressed like boys because—"

"Jane, Jane, Jane." Angela grabbed her forehead and closed her eyes. Jane's behavior was giving her a headache. "Stop insulting these boys. They're going to think—"

"They're *not* boys, Mother." Jane said firmly. "They're girls. Mad and Bec are Maddie and Becca. Girls."

Angela opened one eye and turned it on Maddie and Becca.

"No!" she said as she shook her head. "No girl would ever—"

Maddie and Becca, tired of the need to

always be in disguise, dropped their boyish mannerisms. The result was subtle, but significant. Suddenly, as if by magic, the two boys disappeared and were replaced by two girls dressed as boys.

But Angela wasn't ready for what she saw and shook her head in denial. She knew the truth, could see it with her own eyes, but didn't want to believe.

"Mother…" Jane could see her mother's distress and spoke softly to her. "Girls don't need to be protected. They need to be allowed to vote."

Jane looked at her mother, still in denial, and stood tall. It was time to take a stand.

"My mother always taught me to do what's right," she said, her chin thrust in the air. "Women being able to make decisions for themselves—that's right."

"You're a child, Jane, you don't understand." Angela shook her head sadly as a single tear took the path of least resistance down her cheek. "You need male protection."

"Mother." Jane matured before her mother's eyes as her thoughts became clear. "Don't you want *me* to be able to protect *me*?"

Angela put a hand on each of Jane's shoulders and studied her daughter for several seconds. She liked the strength she saw, the resolve to do what was right. She hugged her daughter tightly before wiping a suspicious wetness from her face. Angela did not cry. And if she did, it was never in public.

"I'll think about it," Angela promised. "Keep an open mind."

Then Angela stepped over to Maddie and Becca. One by one she took each by the chin and gazed at their faces.

"How could I have missed it?" she wondered aloud.

"People see what they expect to see." Becca shrugged.

Angela nodded, took a step back, and looked Becca and Maddie up and down.

"I expect to see a couple of boys acting very ladylike while we're at the capitol," Angela ordered.

"Mother!" Jane complained.

"Fine!" Angela rolled her eyes, but gave in. "But no tears when the ratification fails. If you walk in boys, you have to walk out boys, too."

Becca and Maddie nodded their agreement as Angela locked arms with Jane and the group continued down the street together.

CHAPTER 23

THINGS WERE HOPPING AT the capitol building. Although the legislators had all moved inside to prepare for the vote, the grounds were still packed with protestors, journalists, supporters, and lookers-on.

Most sported either a red or yellow rose. Mostly red.

Angela led the way through the milling crowd, up the steps, and to the door. As she walked, a path cleared before her, which almost always happened. She employed enough families that no one wanted to take a chance they'd offend her. They gladly stepped out of her way.

At the door she paused, conflicted. She truly believed the world would be a much more dangerous place if women were granted the right to vote. The balance of society would be off, and a whole population of uneducated know-nothings would suddenly have their say.

But her daughter had other ideas. Idealistic ideas.

Angela was surprised, really. Jane had never shown the slightest interest in anything but books. Yet for this cause, Angela had seen a real spark of passion.

It was too bad the child was on the wrong side.

Angela thought about denying her help to these strangers she had so spontaneously allowed into her life. There was no real connection to them. It would be amusing to watch them try to swim through this sea of humanity without her help. They were quite likely swindlers of some sort, anyway. No one else would dress up in disguise to dupe innocent people into believing two little girls were boys.

What was the purpose? What did they hope to gain by such a ruse?

Angela turned her head and caught sight of her daughter. Jane had her hand in her pocket, again. She probably had her hand wrapped around that stupid pipe again.

Then Angela noticed the smile on her daughter's face, and the way her child was holding her head tall. Jane had never felt confident enough to hold herself in such a manner before. Angela had worked with her for years and had not succeeded.

Yet suddenly, there was Jane, looking as confident and self-assured as any young lady.

It was those strangers. Potential swindlers or not, Jane was enjoying herself with them, and it was giving her much-needed confidence. Whether Angela liked it or not, the time Jane was spending with them was time well-spent.

Angela straightened her shoulders and turned back to the door as she gave a definitive nod. She schooled her face into a haughty glare and led the way inside. As expected, a pathway melted before her like magic.

Which was fortunate, since the entry hall was filled to capacity, and well beyond. To call it crowded would have been a gross understatement.

A table, staffed by women wearing red roses, had been set up against a wall on the far side of the entry hall. Above the table was a big, bold sign that read *LEMONADE*, Maddie's favorite drink. Maddie spotted it as soon as she stepped into the room.

"Be right back. I'm thirsty," Maddie yelled, and without a second thought she broke away from the group and headed for the table on the opposite side of the room. She and lemonade were old friends and she never passed up an opportunity to get reacquainted with the tasty beverage.

Angela snaked out an arm to stop the child, but Maddie was too quick on her feet. She had worked up a thirst on the walk, and there was lemonade to drink. Her feet might as well have had wheels, she was moving so fast.

"Wait!" Angela yelled.

But Maddie was oblivious to everything but the lemonade.

"Wait here. I'll be right back," Angela yelled over her shoulder and took off after the child.

Angela zigged and zagged through the crowd the best she could, but she had a reputation to uphold. She was hampered by the necessity to maintain a certain level of respectability. Maddie, on the other hand, could care less what anyone thought of her. She was perfectly willing to climb under or over furniture to reach her destination. It was a foregone conclusion that Maddie would reach the table well ahead of Angela.

Which was exactly what happened. Angela panted up to the table just in time to hear Maddie ask, "May I have some lemonade, please?"

One of the three women who were pouring lemonade from pitchers into glass cups looked up at Maddie and frowned.

"Young man, where's your red rose? This lemonade is for those who are true to the cause," the woman scolded.

"Please," Maddie begged. "I'm thirsty!"

The woman's eyes darted about. She needed to find a guard to remove this annoying child from her presence. She had a job to do, and that job was to keep the red rose contingent happy, and in the mood to vote down the ratification. This special lemonade was for supporters of the cause—and supporters of the cause, only.

"Hillary." Angela stepped into her line of sight, placed a hand on each of Maddie's shoulders, and gave a royal nod.

"Angela." Hillary gulped as she returned the nod, hers not at all royal, and added a smile for good measure. The smile took real effort since it was hard to manufacture a realistic-looking smile with her heart fluttering like a trapped butterfly. But she tamped down that irritating fear that always reared its ugly head when any of the bigwigs came around and stretched the corners of her mouth toward her ears.

Angela was most assuredly a bigwig. One of the biggest. Her family employed a good portion of the town, and rumor had it that even though she was just a woman, she could hire and fire at will.

Hillary would do anything to stay in her good graces.

"Is this young gentleman with you?" Hillary asked politely.

"Yes, but...do you have any...umm...fresh lemonade? My friend here is a little young for the kind meant for the legislators." Angela seemed a little uncomfortable for some reason.

Angela's discomfort helped Hillary to relax. It looked like she was going to have an opportunity to curry favor with this powerful woman. Hillary winked to show she understood what Angela wanted, reached under the table, and pulled out a bottle of coke with its unique, hourglass shape.

"I brought along these for those of us who don't want giggle juice," Hillary explained, and she accompanied her words with the biggest wink Maddie had ever seen.

"What...?" Maddie began. She wanted to know what giggle juice was, but when Angela squeezed her shoulders, she recognized it was a signal to keep her mouth shut. She snapped her mouth shut and waited.

"There are five of us." Angela saw that Maddie intended to keep quiet and dropped her hands from Maddie's shoulders. "If you have that many to spare?"

"For your friends, always."

At this point Hillary would have run all the way to the Coca-Cola factory if that was what was needed to do to stay in Angela's good graces, but luckily, she had a stockpile of the beverage on hand. She took out five bottles, opened them, and handed three to Maddie and two to Angela, who both nodded their thanks.

As soon as Maddie and Angela were far enough away from the table that they would not be overheard, Maddie turned to Angela.

"Giggle juice?" she asked.

"Liquor," Angela explained, her face turning brick red. "It's for the legislators. To put them in the right mood so they'll vote down the ratification."

"Wait a minute." Maddie shook her head and her brows came together on her forehead. "What about Prohibition? Isn't alcohol illegal?"

Angela shrugged, but she avoided Maddie's eyes.

"That's not ethical." Maddie's disgust was

clear and present in her tone. "That's—"

But Maddie had overstepped the line. Angela's pride would not allow her to be lectured by a child. Especially not one who dared to glare at her with such disdain.

"I'm not discussing ethics with a ten-year-old girl who disguises herself as a boy," Angela said firmly, once again assuming her royal demeanor.

"I'm disguised because people like you refuse to see my full potential," Maddie countered. "And I'm eleven."

"I don't think—" Angela looked past Maddie to Jane, waiting across the room with Becca and Philip. Jane believed women should have the right to vote. She hadn't had time to discuss this with her child, but she planned to the first chance she got.

She sighed. The world had suddenly gotten much more complicated. She had no energy to argue with this child.

"Do you want to watch the legislators or not?" Angela asked Maddie, her tone crankier than she intended.

Maddie nodded.

"Then let's get the others and head up to the observation gallery."

With that, the argument was over. Angela

and Maddie completed the trek across the entry hall and handed out beverages to their group.

CHAPTER 24

THE GROUP STARTED ON the journey to the balcony together, but almost immediately Angela was intercepted by muckety-mucks from out of town. She motioned to Philip that they should go on without her, and when Jane tried to go with her new friends, Angela took a firm hold of her daughter's arm and held the child tight to her side.

Philip, Maddie, and Becca pushed their way through the milling crowd to the stairs—Philip used his elbows well to clear a path up the stairway—and by the time they reached the door to the balcony all three were thoroughly tired of being human sardines. They were looking forward to finding the perfect place where they could determine what was happening without having their toes stepped on and stepping on toes in return.

Even getting the door to the balcony open was quite the chore. Maddie got there first and had to stomp on quite a few feet to get people to move out of the way so she could crack open the door and look inside. When she saw that the balcony, like every other square inch of the capitol, was full to the brim, she sighed.

"Don't any of these people have jobs?"

"Let me see…" Philip used his elbows to good measure as he and Becca joined Maddie at the door. He looked inside the overcrowded room and shook his head. "Obviously not. Let's go!"

The time traveling trio had traveled through time, hopped freight trains with hobos, and been arrested to get to this time and place. What were a few unruly people in an enclosed space?

Philip manhandled the door open wide enough that the three of them could slip inside. Once they were inside, they worked as a team to shove and stomp their way to the front. It did them no good to be on the balcony if they couldn't see what was happening on the legislative floor.

But when they reached the front, Philip still couldn't tell what was happening. He turned to a man who stood slightly to the side.

"What's the vote?" Philip asked loudly.

"About half have voted. Our side's winning." The man raised a cup of lemonade high in the air and gave a toast. "To our wives and mothers! May they stay in the kitchen where they belong."

A large number of the men in the balcony raised their cups in solidarity.

"Wives and mothers!" they yelled in response. Then in almost perfect synchronization they all took a swig from the cups.

"Looks like they've been practicing," Becca muttered. But she muttered it loud enough that both Maddie and Philip heard her.

Philip sighed as he looked around at the inebriated crowd.

"What do you want to do?" Philip asked. On a balcony with a large group of drunken men didn't seem like the best place for children. And even if they didn't want to admit it, Becca and Maddie were still children.

"We have to talk to Harry Burn," Becca answered. "If we tell him about the letter—"

Becca shook her head. The window of opportunity to fix the timeline was closing and they were no closer to fixing what had been broken than when they first traveled to 1920.

Something needed to be done, and fast!

Philip leaned over the rail to get the layout of the land. Maddie and Becca, on each side of him, followed his lead.

"Guards at all the doors," Philip said. "Even if we could get back to the main level, they'll never let us on the legislative floor to talk to Harry Burn. We need—"

The two sisters locked eyes and nodded. Philip saw the exchange and became worried.

"What's up?" Philip jerked upright so fast it made his head spin. When his eyes focused, he saw that the girls were watching him with interest.

"What I mean is, when you two do that silent communication trick it scares me."

"Not to worry, Philip." Becca put a comforting hand on Philip's arm. Philip didn't trust this gesture of compassion and looked at the hand like it was a tarantula hunting for lunch.

"We've got this." Maddie mirrored Becca's hand-on-the-arm technique. Now Philip was shocked. And even though Maddie's hand was no bigger than Becca's, Philip felt it too was a tarantula, only double in size.

The girls locked eyes and removed their hands from his arms with Swiss watch precision. Philip closed his eyes. He had learned that when those two were synchronized it usually meant trouble. Whatever was coming next, he wasn't likely to enjoy it.

"For Dad," Philip heard Maddie say solemnly.

"For Dad," Becca repeated, just as solemnly.

Philip heard a scraping sound he didn't recognize and opened his eyes to find that both girls had hopped over the balcony and were hanging from the rail. He glanced around at the other inhabitants of the balcony and was shocked to find they were all too far gone to even notice.

"Your mother is not going to like this!" Philip yelled over the rail, furious with himself for not guessing what the girls had planned and hanging on to both of them.

Becca's head popped back up long enough for her to say, "Then don't tell her." Then her head disappeared from sight.

"There's brave, and then there's stupid," Philip muttered. "I'm not sure which this is."

He shook his head, now more disgusted with the girls than himself, and leaned over the rail to see what was going on below.

Rock climbing wasn't much of a sport in 1920, so when the youngsters went over the rail and began to scale down the wall it was something new and unexpected. As soon as they were noticed all other activity stopped immediately. Including the vote.

The sudden silence on the legislative floor became obvious even to the lemonade drinkers in the balcony. Before Philip knew what was happening a large group of them had rushed to the rail to witness this new sporting event. Because that's what it was to the spectators. Before very many seconds had passed, they began to cheer and shout in response to the impressive skill shown by the climbers. Few had seen such an excellent demonstration of proper climbing technique. All were impressed by the climbers' ability to utilize invisible foot and handholds on the flat wall.

The door to the legislative floor slammed open and an army of guards rushed in.

Meanwhile, Angela and Jane, finally free of the muckety-mucks who had monopolized their time, had just that moment arrived on the balcony and squeezed in beside Philip.

"What's happening?" Angela asked as she scanned the legislative floor. She'd never seen this kind of chaos before. Something strange must be happening.

"They're handling things," Philip replied with more sarcasm than he intended.

"Where are Becca and Maddie?" Jane asked after she'd looked around the balcony for the girls and didn't see them.

Philip pointed over the rail at Becca and Maddie, who were climbing across the wall like spiders in their home territory.

Jane leaned over the rail and blinked repeatedly as her brain worked to process what she saw. So intent was she on the drama below that it didn't register when she shoved her hand into her pocket and pulled out her pipe. And no one else noticed, not even her mother, when she popped it into her mouth and began to chew on the stem.

CHAPTER 25

WITH SPIDER-LIKE SKILLS, Maddie and Becca scuttled in a strange zigzag fashion for opposite corners of the wall. The guards below, temporarily confused as their targets headed in opposite directions, finally split into two groups. One followed along below Becca, and the other Maddie.

In the balcony the gamblers of the group were gearing up to make bets. And why not? It wasn't every day a man went to see something as boring as a government vote and had a unique opportunity like this fall in his lap. It was enough to make the adrenaline junkie's heart go pitter-patter. Would a climber fall? Would one or the other of them be arrested before he touched the floor? Which climber would touch the floor first? Would the legislators continue to sit there like lumps, or would they join in on the betting fun?

"Mother, look!" Jane yelled as she hung over the rail to get a better look. "They made it to the ground!"

Angela and Philip each grabbed an arm to keep the excited girl from toppling over the rail. Startled by the feel of her feet leaving the floor Jane opened her mouth to scream, but the scream turned into a groan as the precious pipe, which had been clamped between her teeth, slipped away. In horror she watched as the well-loved pipe tumbled through the air to the legislative floor below where it was lost in the chaos.

As if in sympathy for her loss, the gamblers sent up a groan of monumental proportions. But their groans were the result of the climbers hopping safely down to the floor in perfect synchronization, a result not one of the bettors had thought to predict.

Still, the thrill had been there. It was worth the price of a few dollars to see such a sport. It got the blood flowing. It was good for a man. Money was handed over to the bookies in the crowd and the gamblers relaxed. The exciting sporting event was over. Back to the normal, boring business at hand.

But the sporting event wasn't over for

everyone, at the rail another contender contemplated joining the race to the floor. Only her race would be a solo race.

"I could do that." Jane's face was alight with excitement as she eyed the rail speculatively. Angela's heart skipped a beat at that look. As much as she wanted her daughter to enjoy life and try new things, she drew the line at wall climbing.

"Not in those skirts you couldn't," Angela said firmly. She grabbed a corner of Jane's skirt and gave it a little shake. "You'd trip on this before you got three feet."

But Jane didn't hear her mother. She leaned over the rail to size up the climb to the floor. It didn't look that scary. Not really.

Angela's face drained of color. Jane was seriously thinking of climbing down that wall.

Her pounding heart giving her speed and strength, the mother grasped her daughter's arm and held on tight. Jane's current state of mind was unbalanced—she was entirely too unfettered in her brain to keep her feet firmly on the floor.

Meanwhile, on the legislative floor, the guards were on the run.

One glance at the climbers' trajectory and Sam Smith, the head guard, knew he had them.

He split his squad in half and sent each segment in opposite directions to meet the malcontents where they'd reach ground level.

Smith saw no reason to risk his guards getting hurt by trying to pry those malcontents off the wall. Not that they looked the dangerous type, but it was better to let them reach the floor. One of them might fall and hit someone on the head. They'd be much easier to arrest once their feet were planted firmly on the ground. Plus, after a climb like that, Smith was sure they'd be tired. It would be child's play for his men to scoop them up and march them, double-time, off the legislative floor.

He might even get a commendation for a job well done. Another plaque would look great on his office wall, but what he was really looking forward to was the bonus. Money was always welcome!

Not that Smith did his job purely for the money. He had had a long, successful career dealing with the agitators and ne'er-do-wells who gathered at the capitol. Why these two thought they could cause trouble on his watch was a mystery. He took great pride in the fact that there had never been an incident of any significance while he was on duty. And there never would be.

Smith got a first good look at one of the human spiders' faces and smiled. They were just a couple of youngsters! Boys out for a lark, most likely.

Or, no, this was more likely a dare. Goodness knows he'd been dared to do his share of stupid stunts when he was a boy. And he'd done them, too.

These two were particularly young. Obviously, they were more likely to be mischief-makers than anarchists.

He'd dealt with a lot of mischief-makers in his work. In all his years guarding the capitol, one thing had held true when it came to whippersnappers like these on a lark. It was all fun and games until they were caught. As soon as the pranksters found themselves surrounded by uniforms and billy clubs, even the boldest of them crumpled. They whined and cried like little girls. It never failed.

Smith's plan was a good one, and it would have worked, except for one thing.

The two young climbers who were scaling down the wall weren't there for a dare, or a lark, or to cause mischief. They were on a mission. An important mission.

They had a timeline to fix. A world to make right.

A much-loved dad to save.

There was no crumpling in despair when these spiders hopped to the floor and found themselves surrounded by a veritable wall of manliness intent on stomping on their goals. No, they dived through the column of legs that caged them in and took off across the legislative floor.

They zigged, they zagged, they evaded like trained athletes.

It didn't take long for this new game to be noticed in the peanut gallery, and soon a *whoop* of joy reverberated from the balcony.

The spectators didn't really care what this new sporting event was that was starting up below, they were just reenergized by it. New bets were quickly made, and before long the shouts, moans, and cheers coming from the balcony were even louder and more energetic than before.

Jane, standing beside her mother, immediately joined in the cheering. These were her friends, and it was exciting to watch them race around the legislative floor.

Angela tightened her grip on her daughter and rolled her eyes. The girl was leaning so far over the rail that Angela feared she'd slip and fall.

Philip slammed his fist on the rail. That got Jane's attention and she pulled herself upright to look at him.

"I've got to get down there," he muttered. The girls were his responsibility. He needed to keep them safe, to give them every opportunity to complete the mission.

"Those guards won't let you—" Angela started to say, but Philip was already halfway through the crowded balcony to the door.

"Wait!" she yelled to Philip. "We'll come with you."

Philip reluctantly paused midway to the balcony door.

"We'd better get down there too," Angela yelled to her daughter. She wanted to make sure the girl could hear her over the cheers of the crowd. "They might need us."

Assuming her daughter would follow quietly, like the good little girl Jane had been taught to be, Angela let go of the child and turned to leave. Only, Jane didn't follow. She threw her leg over the rail and the rest of her body would have followed if Angela hadn't snatched her away in time.

"I can do it, Mother," Jane pleaded. "Let me try."

"Not today, Janey." Angela's heart was

pounding out a primal beat of maternal protection for her child. She didn't even want to reprimand the child. All she wanted was to get Jane to safety. After a quick peek over the edge of the rail she pulled Jane into a hug and squeezed tight. "We're using the stairs."

With a firm grip on Jane, Angela dragged her to join Philip, and together they made their way out of the balcony area and down the crowded stairs.

Meanwhile, down on the legislative floor, Becca and Maddie were busy ducking and zigzagging nearer and nearer to Harry Burn, their goal.

Most of the spectators in the balcony had done what was natural to them and chosen a favorite, and excitement was raised to a fever pitch as their favorite kept just out of reach of the guards.

As a sporting event, this one was proving to be surprisingly exciting, and it didn't even cost anything to watch!

Not to be outdone by the spectators in the balcony, several of the legislators relocated to the periphery so they could keep better tabs on the action. They, too, enjoyed a sporting competition, and since they were on the ground floor, so to speak, they wanted to make sure they didn't miss anything. It wasn't long before their shouts could be heard mingling with those of the balcony.

Several times Maddie and Becca were within a few feet of Harry Burn, only to be thwarted by a quickly moving guard who unfortunately chose that spot to make a stand.

On the third attempt to reach the young legislator, Becca thought she would be successful until, out of nowhere, a guard stepped in her way. Becca had no choice but to swerve to the left. Another guard grabbed for Maddie, causing her to swerve right. And with that, the goal suddenly became that much further. Again.

Something had to change. Becca had a brainwave and waved her arms in the air to catch Maddie's attention.

"I'll go high, draw them away. You go low," Becca yelled to her sister.

Maddie nodded her understanding and immediately dove for the floor. One of the spry young guards was about to dive after her until he heard Becca's shout.

"Ha, ha! You can't get me," Becca taunted. It was like she'd waved a scarf in front of a bull or poked a stick in a hornet's nest. Her sister was forgotten as all ire turned to her.

Now that she had their attention, she worked to make herself even more visible. The more they focused on her, the less they would remember her sister. She hopped up on a desk and skipped across the room, using the tabletops as stepping-stones.

The guards gave chase, just as she expected they would, but she easily kept ahead. She was young, nimble, and desperate to succeed.

With the guards busy with her sister, Maddie saw her chance. Keeping under the tables she scuttled, crablike, toward Harry Burn.

"What's wrong?" Becca taunted from across the room when one guard turned Maddie's way. "Too old?"

That angered the guards. Even the young ones.

"Nanny, nanny, boo, boo!" Becca jeered from a tabletop. She put her thumbs to her ears and wiggled her hands about in a way that was sure to annoy. Her plan was to be so irritating that the guards would forget that her sister even existed.

And it worked. The guards were too furious to remember the other boy. They now had one goal, and one goal only.

Catch the rude boy before he made them

look any more useless.

Maddie did her part by staying low and out of sight. Now she was only a few feet from Harry Burn.

Becca, across the room, dove for the ground and rolled. The crowd in the balcony went wild with cheers.

"I can do this, Becca is counting on me," Maddie muttered as she scuttled around several pairs of men's legs and barely missed getting kicked by a legislator who used his feet as well as his mouth when he cheered. She popped her head up to check on her sister's progress just in time to see Becca sprint over a table to avoid a particularly large guard.

Maddie breathed a sigh of relief when she spotted Harry Burn a mere two feet away. No longer caring if she was seen, she jumped to her feet and ran over to him. He looked at her just as a collective gasp from the balcony made Maddie look for her sister.

Horrified, Maddie watched as Becca landed in a heap on the ground.

Maddie's face blanched white and the world swirled dangerously. Everything else forgotten, she rushed, sobbing, to Becca's side. As she knelt and took her unconscious sister's head into her lap, the *bang* of a gavel reverberated through the room like a shot, forcing all eyes to turn to the front of the room where the Speaker of the House stood.

"Recess 'til tomorrow," he shouted, disgust marring his face. "We'll pick up the vote after order is restored."

"Crying like a girl, like they all do," Sam Smith muttered as he looked with pity at the boy who sobbed over his fallen friend. Then he shook his head and motioned to his guards to take the miscreants away.

The guards, their veins no longer flooded with adrenaline, were ashamed they had chased a couple of children around the legislative floor with the same intensity they would have used with hardened criminals. And that shame made them take particular care to be gentle as they lifted Becca from the ground to cart her off the legislative floor.

One of the guards tried to pull the weeping child away, but Maddie's fingers had a death grip on Becca's hand. She had no intention of being separated from her sister.

The guard looked to Smith for instructions but only got a shrug.

Interpreting the shrug to mean *Do what you want*, the guard told the others the two were to stay together.

Tears streamed, unchecked, down Maddie's face as she escorted her unconscious sister. But the tears weren't only for her sister.

What had happened today was worse than a tragic accident.

It was a failure.

CHAPTER 26

NO ONE COULD MISTAKE the room for anything other than it was: an office that some poor fool had unwisely allowed an extra chair to be left in an unused corner. Unwisely, because chairs, like every other creature in the universe, attract their own. Before the dolt knew what had happened, extra chairs from all over the building had migrated to his office and taken up residence in towering stacks that lined each wall. The poor guy tried to get someone to remove the surplus of chairs, but it was a lost cause. He finally gave up and carved out a nice little corner in the records room where he could do his work.

Left on its own, without the oversight of a human occupant, the office quickly became the go-to place for every unwanted item in the capitol. It was to this makeshift storeroom, this home of forgotten items, they took the unconscious Becca.

She lay on a cot once used for influenza victims, in the middle of the room, with a painful-looking bump on the side of her forehead. At the foot of the cot was a worried Maddie, pacing back and forth as she watched her sister's face for any sign that Becca was about to regain consciousness.

After the poor girl had had several minutes to pace, but well before she could wear a hole in the floor, the door opened and in walked an older man with a black leather bag. As soon as she caught sight of the scowl on his face Maddie knew he was of the same vein as a crochety neighbor she'd once had who never failed to yell at any kid who dared to step one foot in his yard.

"I'm Dr. Brown," the man said gruffly as he pointed at Becca. "That my patient?"

Maddie nodded. She looked closely at the doctor's face but couldn't find even a hint of compassion. She decided it would be best if she said as little as possible.

"Family?" he barked, and again he pointed to Becca.

Maddie kept her mouth closed and nodded.

Doctor Brown grunted several times before

he set his bag on the floor next to the door. After looking around he made the unexpected move of grabbing two chairs from a nearby pile and handing one to Maddie. The other he set next to the cot for himself.

"Let's see what we've got here," Dr. Brown muttered as he pried Becca's eye open and used a small flashlight to shine a beam of light into it. He flicked the light around for several seconds as he said nothing, then repeated the process with the other eye.

"Good." The gruff doctor nodded. "No sign of permanent damage."

Maddie watched the doctor's movements closely and became slightly less worried about her sister. While she didn't particularly like the doctor—she had yet to see even a glimmer of empathy—he did seem to know what he was doing.

Dr. Brown studied the bump on Becca's forehead for several seconds.

"That matches the fall I was told he took," Dr. Brown muttered. "Let's see what else we've got."

He gently put his fingers on Becca's head and softly ran his fingers over it, focusing on the back.

"No sign of trauma here." He seemed

pleased with himself, as if he was the reason there was no further trauma on Becca's head. "That means no bumps, bruises, or cuts." Dr. Brown's condescending explanation was aimed at Maddie.

"I know what it means."

Doctor Brown's hands paused at Maddie's answer, then he continued his examination. He looked first in one ear, moved to the other side of the cot, and looked in Becca's other ear. He remained standing for several seconds as his brain processed the data his eyes and fingers had just gathered.

"Ears are fine…no bleeding."

Dr. Brown looked down at his patient. Something wasn't right. He couldn't put his finger on it, but his instincts told him that he was missing something. Something about—

In a flash his brain finished processing the last of the data and it was suddenly clear. He knew exactly what had been worrying his subconscious. Without taking his eyes off Becca's face, he moved back to his chair and sat.

"How old is the patient?"

"Twelve. Almost thirteen."

He flashed a quick, evaluating look at Maddie before nodding to himself. "Have you ever had a bump on the head like this?"

"No."

"Has your sister?"

Maddie froze as Dr. Brown speared her with an intense glare meant to intimidate. And it did intimidate. Every muscle in her body tensed as her automatic fight-or-flight response kicked in and screamed for her to flee. But she remembered her sister, lying unconscious on the cot, and she forced her muscles to relax. She'd never leave her sister behind. Never.

"Thought you had me fooled, didn't you?" The doctor's lip curled in disgust as he looked at Maddie like she was a cockroach that had just crawled across his sandwich.

Maddie's cheeks burned with embarrassment. She tried to control it but couldn't. If a girl's cheeks wanted to blush, blush they would.

"There's more to a boy than just clothes, you know." Dr. Brown's brows came together in a scowl as he lectured. "Or attitude. There's a difference in bone and muscle structure."

"I—"

"Save your breath." Dr. Brown flapped a hand at Maddie dismissively and Maddie's mouth snapped shut. "Let's wake your sister."

Dr. Brown reached for his bag, then

remembered he had left it by the door.

"Mind getting my bag?" Dr. Brown asked Maddie. To make sure she knew it wasn't really a question he tossed his head toward the bag.

Maddie's chin stuck out mutinously as she shook her head negatively.

"Go get it, then, girl," Dr. Brown ordered.

Maddie didn't budge. Dr. Brown opened his mouth to order her to get the bag until he noticed the white-knuckled grip she had on the cot. The death grip, combined with the bulldog-style chin, convinced the doctor to get the bag for himself. Although he did roll his eyes in a surprisingly immature fashion as he stomped to the door.

He grabbed the bag quickly and had turned back toward the cot when the door cracked open, so he missed Jane sliding inside and closing the door softly behind her. And he was too caught up in his own thoughts to notice her hide behind a stack of chairs. He went about his business, making the maximum amount of noise possible each time his foot connected with the floor until he reached the cot, then he dropped his bag with a *thump* on the floor.

"Children today," the doctor grumbled, his nose stuck in the Gladstone bag. "Don't respect their elders like they used to."

He dug into the depths of the bag for several more moments, grumbling all the while. The grumbles blended with the rattle of the instruments to form a low rumble that sounded more like a car engine than human speech.

"They should be ashamed of themselves, using children like this." Dr. Brown pulled his head out of the bag and speared Maddie with a scowl. He shoved his hand into the corner of the bag but kept his eyes on the young girl dressed as a boy. "Lock 'em up and throw away the key. That's what I'd do with the lot of them."

"Who?" Maddie asked, confused. What had she missed while the doctor's head was shoved in the bag and all she could hear was garbled motor sounds?

"Those women. The troublemakers."

"You mean the suffragettes?" Maddie asked.

"Suffragettes, suffragettes." Dr. Brown scoffed. "What a name. Better name would be sufferettes. 'Cause all they want to do is make men suffer."

Dr. Brown's hand touched what he was looking for and his face relaxed from an angry scowl to a concerned frown.

"Men have always taken care of the

women," he explained as he pulled a small vial out of the bag. "It's the way things are. How they should stay. What right do those women have to push their way into men's business?"

He looked from the vial to Becca and seemed to come to a decision.

"This should do it." He nodded as he touched the cap.

"What are you doing?" Maddie yelled. She didn't know what his plans were, but he looked ready to "take care of women" by wiping them from the face of the earth, beginning with her sister.

"Waking your sister with smelling salts. What did you think?"

Dr. Brown uncapped the smelling salts and shoved it in front of Becca's nose. Becca immediately coughed and turned away from the noxious-smelling vial.

Jane, who didn't want to miss anything, shifted forward an inch and dislodged one of the chairs. The entire stack crashed to the floor, leaving her standing in the open with all eyes turned her way.

Dr. Brown turned to Maddie, who was helping Becca sit up in the cot.

"Friend of yours?" he asked with a lift of his brow.

When Maddie nodded, he rolled his eyes.

"More children," he sighed, and he looked as if the weight of the world had suddenly shifted to his shoulders.

He motioned for Jane to approach the cot and she quickly joined her friends.

"She'll be fine. She just needs rest," Dr. Brown assured Maddie as he replaced the vial of smelling salts in his medical bag.

He stood and looked at the three children for a moment. Then his jaw hardened, and a deep anger began to smolder behind his eyes.

"I'll arrange for that," he promised as he closed his bag with a snap.

But when he walked across the room, he had the gait of a man who had lost all confidence in the world. He paused, his hand on the doorknob, and looked back at the children.

"Girls. Dressed like boys. Climbing walls, no less." He shook his head. "Whatever is this world coming to?"

It didn't take an adult to hear the disapproval behind those words. The girls could hear that just fine. But they were too inexperienced to recognize that behind the doctor's words was a distrust of change, a desire to keep the status quo, and a deep disdain for those who would rock the boat.

"You might as well accept it, girls," the doctor growled as previously hidden feelings of frustration bubbled over. "You can't, and never will, be able to do even half of what boys can do."

Maddie and Becca exchanged a look. Dr. Brown intercepted the look and misunderstood.

"It's not just the muscles," Dr. Brown argued. "Girls don't have the brain power for higher thinking. Experiments have proven...*proven*...that women go crazy if they even try to think deep thoughts—"

"Archaic experiments that have been debunked," Becca interrupted. Her head hurt. She didn't feel up to listening to a rant about the inferiority of women.

"Debunked, huh. And archaic." Dr. Brown gave Becca a sideways look. "Mighty big words for a young girl to use."

He stared at Becca much as he would have stared at an alien from space. Then he shook it off.

"As I was saying, women should stay out of men's business. Just look at the mess you girls made today! Tripping over your own skirts—"

"We're not wearing skirts," Maddie

reminded him. She wasn't sure how the doctor could have forgotten that detail. After all, he had just complained that they were dressed as boys.

"Indeed." Dr. Brown paused, flustered. But he wasn't about to give up. "Even worse. You wouldn't find a boy tripping over his pants. Just goes to show females are inferior—"

"I didn't trip. I was pushed," Becca stated flatly as she sat up tall in the cot.

That made Dr. Brown pause for a moment. But only a moment.

"Well, then." He cleared his throat and his eyes swung down to his bag as if it were the most interesting bag in the world. "I'm sure you deserved it."

With those words Dr. Brown twisted the knob and jerked the door open. As he stepped across the threshold, he turned back to the girls to give his parting shot.

"Locked up," he said sternly. "Every last one of them!"

Then he stepped out of the storage room and slammed the door closed behind him. He had had his say. The conversation was done.

CHAPTER 27

THE METAL-AGAINST-METAL *clang* of the cell door slamming shut reverberated through the near-empty cell block of the police station. As the noise faded, heavy footsteps, those of Officer Bobby who was none too pleased to be on jail duty, marched away down the long hallway. Every so often his keys jingled, taunting the three prisoners he had just locked in a single cell with proof he controlled their freedom.

Becca, Maddie, and Jane, the only occupants of the entire cell block, stood silent, their hands clasped to the cold metal bars, as they watched their only connection with the outside world stride away.

The outer door slammed, and the resulting *clang* sliced through the air and severed the fragile heartstrings of the three young girls.

Their hearts dropped to the ground and beat the tune of the jailbird's sad song.

Maddie was the first to pull herself together after the shock of being hauled off and locked up in jail like a hardened criminal. She looked at her sister and sighed.

"Maybe you should rest a little," she said as she pointed to a single, flimsy cot against the back wall. "You took a pretty hard hit to the head."

While Maddie was trying to convince her to rest, Becca scanned the cell for anything interesting. There wasn't much. Until she noticed an old tin cup tucked behind a leg of the cot. She ran to it and picked it up.

"What are you doing?" Maddie asked.

Becca scooted over the bars and gently ran the cup along them. They tinkled merrily.

"Always wanted to do that," Becca mused. Then her face turned mutinous and she used what energy she had to clang the cup hard along the bars. The sound was loud and discordant.

"Bad mistake," Becca moaned as she grabbed her head. "Should have known loud noises would hurt."

Maddie took her sister by the arm and guided her to the cot, leaving Jane alone at the bars.

"I've never been in the pokey before," Jane announced. And with those words she realized she was in the middle of an often-dreamed-of adventure. She turned to her friends and grinned. "What do we do now?"

"Wait for someone to get us out?" Maddie shrugged, unsure if she should be mad that Jane was grinning like this was a game, or happy that the girl didn't seem likely to whine like a baby.

Then she shrugged again and decided it really didn't matter. Maddie turned to her sister to help her get comfortable. She knew there was little chance of success, since the cot was bare of anything so helpful as a blanket or a pillow. It was obvious comfort was not a prime concern in this jail.

∞

Night had fallen and nearly everyone at the capitol building had gone home.

Nearly, but not all.

After hours of frantically searching for the girls with Philip, Angela had finally remembered she had resources at her disposal. She offered a reward for information about the whereabouts of Jane and the two "boys," any information, and soon Nashville was awash with a flood of searchers looking for the missing children.

Random sightings and rumors were all that had been brought to Angela so far, but she paid for each tidbit no matter how small or inconsequential it was. Someone was sure to find something relevant soon. When they did, she wanted them to bring the information straight to her as fast as their feet could carry them.

Now it was a waiting game. Angela and Philip had planted themselves in the center of the walkway—it was a central location with a view of the most ground—amid discarded picket signs and rose petals. By far the most abundant items were the rose petals, which littered the ground like a thick dusting of yellow and red snow.

"We should have news soon," Angela said for at least the twentieth time. Then, because she wasn't the type to twiddle her thumbs as she waited for word that her daughter was safe, she reached down and dug through the discarded petals until she found two perfect petals, one yellow and one red. She held them up for Philip to see.

"Strange," she mused. "They're equally beautiful."

Then, the momentary distraction over, she crushed the petals in her hands. She showed the resultant mess to Philip.

"And equally fragile," Angela said, and her words seemed to have hidden meaning.

Angela dropped the petals to the ground but the red one plopped onto her shoe. She kicked it away angrily, then looked Philip in the eye.

"Even if the ratification fails, the world will never be the same, will it?" Angela kicked again, sending a cloud of a red and yellow into the air.

"Do you want it to be?" Philip used both hands to scoop up a handful of petals. He lifted them high into the air before he released them and watched as they danced and floated to the ground.

"I want Jane to be safe. Protected. During the war I thought—"

But what Angela thought during the war would have to wait, as a boy darted across the grounds to whisper in her ear. Angela nodded and put a kind hand on his shoulder.

"You've done well, Michael." She nodded. "I'll make sure you're well rewarded."

The boy smiled happily as he ran off.

Angela showed no sign of her thoughts as she watched the child until he was out of sight. Then she turned to face Philip.

"They're in jail," she stated bluntly.

"Jail!" Philip's voice rose in anger. That was the last thing he expected to hear. "They're children. What kind of barbaric—?"

"Calm down, Philip, I'll get them out," Angela assured him. "My daughter does not belong in a cage. Anyone who puts her in one—"

Before Angela could expand on the punishments that awaited those who dared to cage her daughter, Philip grabbed a large yellow rose, which was wilted almost beyond recognition, and handed it to Angela.

"What's this for?" she asked, confused.

"I think you just switched sides."

"What—?"

Angela looked at the wilted yellow rose in her hand, then around her at the multitude of pro-ratification signs stacked nearby.

"I don't..." she began, but her words stuck in her throat when she noticed one of the signs depicted a man releasing a woman from prison with a key labeled *19th Amendment*.

"Oh, dear!"

Angela's eyes widened as a tidal wave of

new ideas annihilated a lifetime of old ones. A paradigm shift can be a traumatic experience, and as the blood left her face and she became a ghost of herself, Philip braced to catch her.

But Angela was not the fainting kind and it only took a moment for the dead white to be replaced by a painful, deep red. Philip had had enough embarrassments in his life that he knew exactly what that burning red meant.

"Get the girls," Philip suggested kindly. "I'll work on getting that letter back."

Angela nodded in agreement and watched as Philip strode down the walkway and out of sight. Then she took a deep breath, lifted her chin, and headed to the police station.

CHAPTER 28

THIRTY MINUTES LATER ANGELA, arms crossed, stood behind a sweating Officer Bobby as he jiggled a set of keys in the lock of the cell. He was nervous and worried—and Jane, Maddie, and Becca were crowding the door, waiting for it to open, did nothing to make the situation better.

"This is how the police use our tax dollars? Arresting children?"

Officer Bobby made no response to Angela's question as he tried a second key.

"And what's taking you so long with this lock?" Angela's voice was set to maximum stern level and reminded Officer Bobby of his own mother when he had done something naughty or stupid. "What if there was an emergency?"

Officer Bobby jiggled the keys around so he

could try a third key. His shoulders melted with relief when the lock clicked into place and the door squeaked open.

Jane was the closest to the opening, so as soon as the door swung open a crack, she shoved through and ran into her mother's arms. Officer Bobby quickly slammed the door closed and relocked it, leaving Maddie and Becca inside.

"Are you okay, darling?" Angela was squeezing her daughter so tight the girl couldn't have answered even if she wanted. Luckily, she didn't want to answer, she just wanted to go home.

When Angela had had a good, long, mother's hug, she held Jane at arm's length and studied her face. Jane had been the object of that worried, conflicted look many times in her life and something about it had always confused her. It was as if her mother had a secret, a secret about Jane, that she never planned to tell.

Jane sighed. She was too tired to worry about *the look*, as she called it to herself.

"I'm fine," Jane reassured her mother.

Angela continued to study her child's face for several seconds more, then gave a satisfied nod. She turned her attention to the two children who were still behind bars.

"And you two?"

"We're fine," Becca answered for both sisters. "Where's Philip—"

Angela raised a hand to silence Becca. She pulled her shoulders back until she was ramrod straight, tilted her chin in the air so she could look down her nose at Officer Bobby—which was the proper method for full aristocratic mode—and addressed the young policeman.

"I'll be taking my daughter home now. I'll take these two also. Open the door," Angela ordered.

"Can't do that, ma'am. My orders are to release your daughter, and only your daughter. The boys gotta stay locked up."

Officer Bobby pulled on his collar. He was in a tough place and he knew it. If he didn't follow orders, his career could be over. But he had been told that this woman's family wielded a lot of power in the town. Which meant ignoring her orders might have the same effect.

Angela watched the play of emotions on Officer Bobby's face and relaxed. It looked like the autocratic mode wouldn't be needed after all. She smiled kindly at the young officer.

"Do you have...ambition, officer?" Angela asked, for all the world like she was honestly interested. "Do you plan a career in policing?"

"Yes, ma'am." Officer Bobby gulped. He did not trust this sudden friendliness.

"A fine young man like you could go far. With the right backing." Angela reached over and flicked at his uniform. Officer Bobby looked down and saw that it was the insignia that designated his low rank that she had flicked. He blushed.

Angela nodded at that blush. She had suspected that this young man's Achilles' heel would be his ambition. It was nice to see that her business acumen was useful for more than boardroom meetings and acquisition negotiations.

"Jail duty's not much fun, is it?" She shook her head in sympathy. "I bet you'd like to be in the action."

Officer Bobby watched her, unsure where she was going with this.

"Those two," Angela said sweetly as she pointed at Maddie and Becca, still behind bars, "are my daughter's friends. I want to take them home with me."

"They'll have to stand trial, ma'am." Officer Bobby stiffened his back as he shook his head. This woman was being too nice to have any real power behind her. He'd best follow his boss's orders and stay out of trouble. "What they did was—"

"Was what?" Angela interrupted, but her voice remained gentle. "Stupid? Juvenile?"

Angela let go of her daughter and stepped over to the cell. She reached through the bars and gently cupped Maddie's chin. Maddie, who was a quick thinker, smiled like an angel. It was obvious to her the part she was to play.

"Look at this face. Is this the face of a criminal?"

Officer Bobby looked at Maddie's young face, which somehow reminded him of a Kewpie doll his sister had adored and played with for hours on end. But even though Officer Bobby was at the beginning of his career, he'd been around long enough to know that an innocent smile didn't necessarily guarantee innocence.

"I'd lose my job," he said mulishly, unwilling to risk his career for two young hoodlums who'd probably end up back in jail in a week.

"What if—?"

Angela's brain raced frantically. What could she offer this young man that would sway him to her way of thinking? Then, she had it.

"What if the department gets a new motorcar?" Angela lowered her voice to a conspiratorial whisper. "Tomorrow. With the stipulation that you drive it?"

"Me? A car?" Officer Bobby's eyes dilated at the thought.

"The newest model. It would mean a promotion," Angela told him, just in case he was unaware. "And all you have to do is release two harmless children into my custody."

Officer Bobby was a young man out to make good in his chosen career. Angela's bribe was the right combination of good for him, and for the department. He quickly pulled the keys out of his pocket, and this time it only took one try for him to click the lock open so he could release the prisoners. Maddie and Becca hightailed it out of that hated cage so fast he barely had time to step out of their way.

"Well done, Officer." Angela nodded. "You've got a good career ahead of you."

Officer Bobby watched as Angela and the jailbirds walked down the long hallway to the exit. When they were safely through the door, he went into the cell and straightened everything, making it look as if no one had even been there. As he stepped out of the cell he shrugged.

"At least I hadn't done the paperwork yet. Makes it that much easier."

He clanged the cell door closed and smiled.

"Me," he mused, "driving a police car!"

He whistled a few bars as he began the long walk down the hallway to the exit, then he had a better idea. He pulled his night stick out of his belt and ran it along the bars of the cell as he passed.

"Just like a xylophone," he said, satisfied.

Today had been a good day.

CHAPTER 29

BY THE TIME THE jailbirds stepped into the parlor at Angela's house they were exhausted.

Angela could tell they were exhausted because the entire way back all three of them complained about how tiring being locked up in the big house was, and they only perked up when they saw the sofas and chairs of the parlor. Then it was a race to see who got which resting place, followed by a convincing reenactment of marathon runners collapsing after crossing the finish line.

Angela thought of closing the doors and letting the children sleep, until Becca popped up and asked, "Where's Philip?"

"He's fine. He had something he needed to do." Angela reassured her.

Becca leaned back slowly. She was honestly tired. Maybe it was the bump on the head.

Angela did a visual check of each of the girls to make sure there were no noticeable bumps or bruises—other than Becca's head, of course—then tiptoed over to her daughter.

"Tired?" she softly asked Jane.

"There was only one cot, and it wasn't very comfortable," Jane answered with a yawn.

"It probably wasn't meant to be." Angela paused a moment, then said in the serious type of voice no child ever wants to hear, "We need to talk."

She sat in a chair near Jane and gently took the girl's hands. At her touch, Jane's eyes popped open in surprise. Rarely did her mother look anything but strong. But sitting on the edge of her chair with her head lowered meekly she looked...well, beaten.

"I'm sorry you girls got mixed up in this," Angela whispered softly. "Especially you, Jane."

"Mother, I—"

"No, don't try to make me feel better." Angela raised her head and Jane's breath snagged in her throat when she recognized failure in her mother's eyes.

"It's my job to protect you," Angela continued, "and—"

"I thought it was Granddad's job." Jane pulled her hands away from her mother. She had never seen this side of her mother before, but she was sure she didn't like it. "And Uncle James's job."

Angela opened her mouth to speak several times but had trouble finding the words. Finally, she spoke.

"Well. As your mother I—"

"Have no rights over your own children," Jane interrupted. "Or property. Or the right to start a business. Or—"

"Jane! What's gotten into you?"

What had gotten into Jane was fear. Her mother had always been the strongest and smartest person she knew. The woman who always knew exactly what needed to be done, and who did it without hesitation. The woman who was an unbreakable rock who could be relied on, no matter what.

And yet, at the first sign of her daughter in trouble, the woman had fallen apart. And for what? Because Jane had spent a few measly hours in jail? The mother of an adventurer—and Jane was even more determined than ever to be an adventurer—needed more backbone than that.

Jane looked from Maddie and Becca, who were watching with interest, to her mother's horrified face. She made a quick decision and sprang from her chair.

"I want to show you something," she blurted as she raced through the door and up the stairs.

Angela wasn't feeling much like her usual confident self, and she didn't like it. Her eyes fell on the two girls, dressed as boys and lounging about like they hadn't a care in the world, and she realized everything had been fine until they showed up. So, when a flicker of anger sparked toward the two children, instead of stomping it out of existence like she'd normally do, she let the fire feed on past frustrations, and it grew into a full-fledged bonfire.

"She's never spoken to me that way before." Angela glared at the two children. "What did you do to her?"

"Nothing." Maddie shook her head. "We just talked about—"

"You brainwashed her!" Angela still had enough control not to yell, but barely. "You took advantage of her because she's a child—"

"She's a year older than me," Becca interrupted.

That one argument was enough to pour a bucket of cold water on the bonfire of anger. Angela paused a moment, unsure what to do with the final, hot coals of anger that made her heart uncomfortable.

"Doesn't matter," Angela sputtered. "She's been protected."

Angela looked pointedly at Becca's and Maddie's feet.

"Are your shoes dirty?"

Becca and Maddie, not sure of the answer to that question, looked down. Maddie brushed away a twig and a clump of dirt as Becca answered, "No."

Angela noticed the dirt but decided to ignore it. She honestly didn't care about the dirt. She just needed to blow off a little more steam.

Calmer now, Angela waited uncomfortably with the two girls for Jane's return. But she still didn't feel much like herself and couldn't sit patiently, so she gave twiddling her thumbs a try. It wasn't very satisfactory.

"Where is that girl?" Angela asked, not really expecting an answer.

"That girl" was in her bedroom—a very well-appointed bedroom full of everything a girl could want, searching through every drawer.

"Where did I put them?"

Jane sat back on her heels and looked around. She wasn't a very organized person. If she wanted to hide something, she usually stuck it wherever was most convenient. She rarely thought about having to find it again.

But she knew it was in this room. Where would she put the things?

"The chest!"

Jane raced across the room to a toy chest. After lifting the lid, she tossed dolls, blocks, and toy trains into a pile until she could reach the bottom where she'd stashed the stack of pamphlets. She held them tightly in her arms and rushed out of the room to head back downstairs.

Meanwhile, in the parlor, Angela had gotten tired of twiddling her thumbs. Since she was still a little hot under the collar, she turned her glare on Maddie, the owner of the clump of dirt plopped unceremoniously on her otherwise pristine floor.

"You know what she wants to show me, don't you?" Angela asked. It was more of an accusation than a question.

"No, ma'am," Maddie replied meekly. She had seen Angela's eyes focus on the clump of dirt and felt guilty.

The meek and polite response softened Angela, but just a bit.

"At least one of you has manners."

Angela turned her glare on Becca. She was

about to find something about the girl to critique when Jane shot into the room, her hands full of pamphlets.

"I paid for them to be printed, Mother," Jane said as she dumped the stack of pamphlets in her mother's lap. "Out of my allowance. I've been supporting the cause for over a year."

Angela slowly looked through the pamphlets. They were pro-suffrage. She was shocked, but mostly because these pamphlets made her realize she didn't know her daughter as well as she thought she did.

"Jane!" she gasped. She searched her daughter's face, looking for the child who had always looked at her with blind adoration. What she saw was a budding young woman with a mind of her own.

"Women should be allowed to vote, Mother." Jane's chin jutted out stubbornly. "It's time."

"Do you mind?" Angela suddenly felt old at the thought of such a grown-up daughter. She turned to Becca and Maddie. "I'd like to speak to my daughter in private."

"Let's find Philip," Becca suggested to Maddie.

Maddie, who had become uncomfortable with the mother/daughter drama that was unfolding, nodded. The two sisters slammed the front door on their way out.

As soon as Angela knew they were alone she turned to Jane.

"Jane, dear," she said softly, much as she had talked to the girl when she was two. "You're still a baby. You shouldn't worry—"

"I'm not a baby, Mother."

The impeding argument was cut short by a loud knock on the front door, followed by an obvious scuffle. Before they could do more than look at each other Douglas Whitfield appeared in the parlor doorway straightening his clothing.

With a glare behind him—most likely at the butler whose job it was to keep out the riff-raff—Douglas stepped into the parlor and closed the doors firmly behind him.

"Mr. Whitfield?" Angela raised an expressive eyebrow at his boldness.

Ignoring the implied question, Douglas sauntered over to Angela and grabbed one of the pamphlets from her hands.

"There's a traitor among us, I see." Douglas smirked. "I knew you couldn't be trusted. Not when someone so close to you is batting for the other side."

It had been a rough, emotional day. First,

she had discovered she might be on the wrong side of the ratification fight, then she had to bribe a policeman to let her daughter out of jail, and finally she found out that her daughter had been going behind her back to support a cause Angela was against, for an entire year!

It was time to tell Jane why she had not been allowed to go to school with other children. No doubt about it. When Jane was younger it was necessary to keep secrets for her protection, but recent events had shown that the girl was growing up.

Angela had dreaded this day for years and had just steeled herself to have a long talk with Jane when this man, this Douglas Whitfield, bulldozed his way into her parlor and called her a traitor.

It was almost more than she could take. Her brain was too tired to deal with anything else.

What was this man doing in her house, anyway? And why was he treating her like she was...she was...like she was his secretary!

"Sit down. I need to talk to your mother."

Angela looked up in time to see Douglas pin Jane with a glare and motion to the sofa. Then she saw Jane meekly sit.

How dare that man order her daughter about in such a cavalier manner! He had no right, no right at all!

Angela sat up ramrod straight and lifted her head high. And although she wasn't really looking down her nose at him—that would have been physically impossible since he stood, and she sat—she certainly gave that impression.

"May I help you?" Her voice hit the subzero range in true ice queen fashion.

"You certainly can."

Angela, not wanting to waste her precious breath on this lowly creature, simply raised a queenly brow.

"You can come down off your throne and put the pressure on." Douglas nodded toward her brow. "Use your money. Make sure the red roses carry the day."

Angela looked at Jane, who pleaded with her eyes as she pointed to the pamphlets. Then the girl did several little gyrations that Angela took to mean *Please don't make any promises*.

"It would be best for your daughter."

Angela's eyes flew to Douglas.

"Is that a threat?" she asked, her eyes knives pointed at his head.

"Not in the way you think." Douglas seemed impervious to Angela's dagger eyes, which is something that had never happened to Angela before. "It's just, what man would want a wife...?"

Douglas stopped speaking long enough to reach into his pocket and pull out a stack of letters tied with a bow. That Angela recognized those letters was obvious by the way all the color drained from her face.

Jane, unused to seeing her mother at a disadvantage, leaned forward. What would her mother do? How would she put this man in his place?

"Whose mother—"

Douglas separated one envelope from the stack, took the letter out, and read it.

"Hot stuff," he snickered as he flapped the letter in the air in front of Angela's face, nearly hitting her on the nose in the process. "Newspapers are going to eat this up."

Angela blanched even whiter, if that was possible, then her cheeks infused with an angry red. She snatched at the letter.

But Douglas was on his feet, while Angela was sitting. That put him at an advantage. All he had to do was take a step back and the letter was out of her reach.

Angela, frustrated, snatched at it again, and again the man easily kept it out of her grasp. Soon the two were playing a strange version of keep away in which Angela tried to maintain her ice queen pose while snatching wildly at the letter.

Jane, perched on the edge of the sofa cushion, was conflicted. As much as she was curious about those letters—she hadn't known there was anything in the world that could upset her mother so completely—it worried her that her strong, always-in-control mother was distraught.

"How dare you!" Angela croaked.

Now Jane was truly worried. Angela never did anything so lowly as to croak. She had always taught Jane that anything other than a calm, well-modulated tone of voice was crass and uncouth. It wasn't done in their circle.

Jane was confused by this whole situation. One minute Angela was normal, self-assured and in control, the next, she was at the mercy of this man. What was in those letters?

"Give me my letters." Angela still sounded like a demented frog. "Those are private property."

"Women. Always so weak."

Douglas snickered as Angela's haughtiness finally deserted her completely. She bounded to her feet and tried to snatch the letter out of Douglas's hand. When that failed, she grabbed for the stack of letters in his other hand. Soon she was jumping about in what she would consider a very unladylike fashion. And it did no good. Douglas was quite a bit taller and had no problem keeping all the letters out of her reach.

"How did you get those?" Angela stared at the letters with a strange combination of hunger and loathing.

"I'm not one to leave things to chance." Douglas took his eyes off Angela long enough for a quick look at the letters. "As soon as I discovered your daughter was helping the other side, I realized I needed leverage."

"Those are private property!" Angela tried to pull herself together to infuse her voice with its usual authority, but it was a lost cause. She felt too vulnerable.

"Then you should have kept them in a safe, instead of the bottom drawer of your dresser."

Angela sank into a nearby chair, defeat writ large on every fiber of her being.

Jane sat back as her face paled with fear. This man, this interloper, had defeated her mother. The same woman who had always taken care of her and kept her safe. The same women that she had thought of as the strongest person in the world.

"How…how dare you!" Angela was trying for haughty but could only manage desperate.

"I dare a lot, if it's important enough," Douglas explained calmly. "And women *cannot* be allowed to vote."

Angela's eyes pleaded for mercy. The destiny of her child was in the hands of this man, this stranger. She had no control, no control at all.

Then it hit her. She was acting weak and vulnerable, exactly like those women she so often condemned. She, with all the wealth she could ever need to back her up, brought down by a stack of letters.

Maybe if she talked to this man, calmly, she could reason with him. After all, she ran her family's businesses every day. She often had to deal with men who wanted to show her less respect than she deserved.

She took a deep breath, then calmly sat on the edge of the chair with her back ramrod straight.

"Why is it so important to you?" she asked, for all the world as if it was of no importance.

Douglas looked at Angela, unsure where all this sudden calmness came from. But he wasn't worried. He had all the leverage he needed right here in his hands. He smoothed out the open letter, which had refolded as it waved about in the air.

"Let's just say it would mess up all my plans." Douglas smirked as he looked over the letter. Angela's face turned beet red at the thought of what he must be reading. "Who needs the extra competition?"

Then, with all the showmanship of a stage magician, Douglas refolded the letter, put it back in its envelope, and slid the envelope under the bow.

Angela watched as he put the entire stack back in his pocket.

"It would ruin everything," he said, more to himself than to Angela.

Angela licked her lips. Her face remained calm, even though inside she was scrambling.

"How did you find out about them?" she asked as casually as she could manage. "No one alive except me knows about those letters."

"I'm a curious person." Douglas shrugged, for all the world like spying on people was a normal thing. "And you folks aren't very good at closing curtains. Anybody with an ounce of curiosity could watch you for hours and hours."

Angela shivered at the proof that her privacy had been invaded. She lifted her chin a touch higher. It was time to regain control of the situation.

"I'll call the police," she stated, and this time, the first since she caught sight of those letters, her voice was calm and controlled.

Jane sat up. She had not thought of the police. It was illegal to steal personal property and threaten to reveal that personal property. One was called theft, and the other blackmail.

"Go ahead," Douglas replied, seemingly unconcerned.

But Jane didn't hear his unconcern because she was too busy sneaking out of the room. As she slammed the front door, she paused just long enough to grab the pipe out of her pocket and pop the stem into her mouth. She'd never had reason to go to the police for help before. The pipe would give her the courage she needed to perform such a task.

Back in the parlor, the slam of the door had caught Douglas's attention. He looked around the room and noticed Jane was missing.

"Where's she going?" he asked.

"For the police, most likely." Angela still sat tall and straight. "Jane—"

But Angela got no further as Douglas pulled the packet of letters back out of his pocket and flapped them in the air.

"Nice." Douglas was pleased with himself.

"The police will find these stimulating reading. I'm sure they'll see you in a new light after this."

Douglas snickered and smirked.

"It will *color* their view of you, I'm sure."

Angela's cheeks flamed red as she melted into the chair, defeated. She couldn't let anyone else read those letters. They were too personal.

Douglas, an old pro at manipulation, noticed the exact moment Angela gave up. He switched gears and turned on the charm.

"Look," he said, for all the world as if his fondest wish was to do Angela a favor. "The last thing I want to do is hurt you or your family."

Angela looked at her would-be blackmailer, and Douglas could see the glimmer of hope spark in her eyes. He had her exactly where he needed her.

"I just want what is mine to stay mine," he explained. "To do that, the Nineteenth Amendment must fail."

"But I don't understand what you want from me!" Angela's frustration was obvious. "I already support the antis!"

"You have so far," Douglas explained. "But you're slipping. I can see it. Your heart isn't in it anymore."

Douglas pointed to the pamphlets, which had been tossed on the couch.

"There's the proof your daughter has been corrupted. How far can you be?"

Angela shrugged. Deep in her heart she knew Douglas was right. She had lost the will to fight against ratification.

CHAPTER 30

SERGEANT JONES WAS TIRED. Not a-full-day-of-work tired, where a person could go home, get some shut-eye, and be ready for more action the next day. No, he was bone tired. Soul tired. Tired of spending all day, every day, chasing criminals, writing tickets, and doing what he was told.

But it was more than that. He was done. He was ready to spend his days fishing, sitting on the porch, sleeping late, and eating a big breakfast. Just not particularly in that order, of course.

Luckily his bosses had noticed his excessive lethargy and had put him on desk duty until his scheduled retirement date, which was only a few months away. For the safety of the good citizens of Nashville, and the sanity of everyone who had to work with him.

To make things even easier they had him on the night shift. His duties included lounging with his feet up behind the counter for a few hours and taking a stroll through the precinct every so often. It worked well because no one ever came to the precinct at night. All the good citizens of the city were cozy in their homes. All the bad ones, the criminals who were up to no good, made sure to keep well away from the station.

Sergeant Jones got out his paper and propped up his feet on the desk. It was newspaper time, his favorite time of the day. He could read to his heart's content with no one to bother him. He could catch up—

Jane burst through the door like a tornado on steroids and her momentum carried her all the way to the counter. There she stood, panting from the effort of her run, hair messy and windblown, the front of her dress muddy from where she tripped on a curb and fell, and that old pipe still stuck in her mouth.

"What's this now?" Sergeant Jones asked. But though the words were a question, there was no question in his body language. As crazy as it was for a whirlwind to blow into the precinct at this time of night, Sergeant Jones barely looked Jane's way and he certainly didn't take his feet down. Not when it was newspaper time.

It was quite a distance from Jane's house to the police station and Jane had run the entire way. She wanted to speak, she truly did. But she was huffing and puffing like a steam engine and her lungs hurt too much for her brain to form any words. Every time she opened her mouth to say something, no words came, and she looked like a fish out of water. She needed a minute, and a couple hundred gulps of air.

But Sergeant Jones had no desire to let her catch her breath. Because as tired as he was, he was still a police officer. And she might have a problem he'd need to solve.

"Go home, little girl," Sergeant Jones said dismissively. "You don't belong here."

"My mother—" Jane managed to huff out the words.

"Should've raised you right," Sergeant Jones interrupted gruffly. "If a man tells you to go home, you go home. No backtalk."

"But—"

"Leave!" Sergeant Jones yelled. He kept his eyes firmly on his paper but used his left hand to point to the door.

Jane bit down on her pipe in frustration. Her mother wasn't the yelling kind, and few others would dare to yell at a child of the richest family in town, so she was in unchartered territory.

Her breathing calmed as she wrestled with the dilemma of what to do. She looked at the policeman, who continued to read his paper and ignore her existence. She shuffled her foot around a bit, trying to get his attention, but it was no good. He ignored her the same way he'd ignore an ant carrying a breadcrumb across the room.

She was defeated. This man would never listen to her, so how could she convince him that her mother needed help?

As she turned to walk back to the door, she spotted a trash basket against the wall full of pamphlets. Pro-ratification pamphlets. Her feet changed course and she ran to the bin to grab one from the top of the pile. It was one of the ones she had funded, the one that had *EQUAL RIGHTS FOR WOMEN* written in large, bright, yellow letters.

It was one of her favorites. And here it was, in the trash.

"What's this?" she asked as she turned back to Sergeant Jones.

Sergeant Jones, who had been deep in a story about fly fishing and had forgotten about the girl, looked up and saw the pamphlet in her hand.

"Where have you been?" He returned to his paper, uninterested. "Trash like that is all over the city."

Jane stared at the pamphlet as the gears in her brain turned at a frantic rate. This moment, this experience of her at the police station asking for help and being ignored, was a perfect example of why the Nineteenth Amendment must be ratified.

Because deep in Jane's heart she knew she wasn't being ignored so much because she was a child, as because she was a female.

"Be a good girl and go home." Sergeant Jones flapped a dismissive hand in her general direction. "Stop bothering me."

The gears in Jane's head clicked into place and she knew what she had to do. She dropped the pamphlet in the trash, straightened her shoulders, and turned to face Sergeant Jones.

"My mother," Jane said in a surprisingly calm voice, "needs help. There's this man—"

"Didn't you hear me, girl?" Sergeant Jones growled, his feet still on the desk and his eyes glued to the newspaper. "I said go home!"

"My mother needs help!" Jane yelled. If calm didn't work, maybe irate would.

"Eh!" Sergeant Jones, unimpressed by Jane's

yells, again flapped a hand in her direction. "If I called the boys out every time a little girl worried about her mommy, I would've been kicked off the force years ago."

Jane's life to date had been a pampered one. Whatever she wanted she usually got. She didn't know how to deal with the frustration she felt so she clamped down, hard, on the stem of her pipe and cracked it.

Sergeant Jones heard the crack and knew exactly what it meant. He smoked a pipe and had himself cracked a stem or two in times of stress.

"Ah, poor little girl's mad." He smirked. "Go home and wash a dish or something. That'll make you feel better."

Jane stood perfectly still as she struggled to tamp down her feelings like she had seen her grandpa tamp the tobacco into his pipe. She'd seen her mother in many confrontations, but until tonight she'd never seen her scared, frustrated, or angry.

Her mother approached every challenge with an impressive calmness. It was one of the reasons she was so successful in business. She never let anyone get under her skin.

Jane decided she'd do the same and calmly took the pipe out of her mouth and stuck it in her pocket.

She walked slowly to the counter—she channeled her mother's haughtiness for good measure—and stood looking at Sergeant Jones. She did nothing else, just looked at the man as if he were a bug she might need to squish.

"What?" he asked, unable to ignore the weight of her eyes.

Jane, for the first time since she entered the precinct, had the upper hand. She didn't say a word. She simply looked at the man.

Few people can stand the effects of a full-on stare. Particularly when that stare is accompanied by a you-are-a-bug look.

Sergeant Jones certainly couldn't. He stood up so fast his feet banged to the floor and his newspaper fell into the trash.

"Why don't you just go home?" he roared.

"Why don't you do your job?" was Jane's calm rejoinder.

Sergeant Jones glared at Jane, putting the full weight of his superior sex and age behind that glare.

Jane remained unfazed. She stood tall with her chin high as she gazed at Sergeant Jones. It was clear she thought him a strange creature barely worth her time.

The test of wills between the man and the girl went on for several minutes, until Sergeant Jones admitted defeat. He gave himself a little shake, then sauntered as casually as he could manage over to the counter and picked up a pencil.

"Fine!" he sighed. "I'll call the boys out if it'll make you happy."

Jane nodded regally.

"Where should I send them?"

Sergeant Jones put pencil to paper, and his face turned brick red as he took down the information Jane gave him.

It was a good thing he was a conscientious police officer who took the time to listen to this girl. Otherwise, he might have found himself kicked off the force with no pension.

CHAPTER 31

BACK AT THE MANSION ANGELA was in obvious distress. Gone was her ramrod-straight back, gone was her haughty attitude, and most importantly, gone was the last shred of her composure. She was a mess.

Douglas stood over her with the stack of letters in his hand while she curled in the chair in a semi-fetal position.

"He was the love of my life." Angela's words were nearly drowned out by the tears that streamed down her face. "We wanted to marry, but it was against the law. We—"

"Mother, wait!" Jane yelled from the doorway.

Angela forced her eyes to focus and discovered her daughter had returned and had brought help. She was flanked by a policeman on each side.

"That's the man," Jane said, turning to the cop on her right. "Take him to the pokey."

She looked quickly at her mother to see if she had noticed the slip. But Angela was busy using her sleeves to wipe the tears from her face, so obviously not.

"I mean, arrest him!" Jane pointed dramatically at Douglas Whitfield.

Douglas was determined to play it cool. He shoved the letters into his jacket pocket and turned a smiling face to the two policemen, who had stepped closer to him.

"Gentlemen." He gave each of them a friendly nod. "How may I help you?"

The policemen were confused. They had been sent here to help a woman, most likely the one bawling her eyes out on the chair.

But the man appeared to belong to the house. He certainly acted like he was in charge. If that was the case, he had every right to reprimand his womenfolk and keep them in line.

Sergeant Jones was going to hear about this. The force wasn't meant for domestic squabbles. They had no desire to interfere with what went on between a man and his wife. Men had the right to run their homes how they saw fit. Rights that needed to be protected.

The officers exchanged a look and stepped back to the doorway. Douglas smiled at them and turned back to Angela.

"You have a commitment to the cause." He patted the pocket with the packet of letters. "Your daughter's future depends on it."

With that threat left hanging in the air Douglas sauntered to the doorway and gave a nod to the officers who stood in his way.

"Gentlemen." They had not moved out of his way, so he raised a brow for good measure.

The officer to the right stepped aside, giving Douglas a clear path to freedom. He had only taken a single step before he was stopped by a hand on his arm. He looked down and saw that the hand belonged to that brat of a kid, Jane. He had a good mind to toss the child aside—he didn't like people who got in his way—but he feared any action against the daughter would break the hold he had over the mother.

"You have something that belongs to my mother," Jane accused, for all the world like she was a store owner and had caught Douglas shoplifting.

Douglas sneered at the child. She clearly didn't realize the hold he had over her mother. He turned to Angela and looked down his nose at her, the threat of doom implicit in his sneer.

He was sure the woman would order her out-of-control spawn to move aside and let him pass.

But Angela was done crying, and she was done allowing this man to intimidate her. Her daughter had shown real strength here. It was time for Angela to pull herself together and take charge. She uncurled and sat up straight.

"Officers." Angela licked her lips and tried to act confident, but her voice was still shaky from all the crying. "This man is a thief!"

The officers weren't sure who to believe. Was the man a thief, or the homeowner?

Douglas was confident he could talk his way past the cops—he'd done it many times before. And he might have succeeded this time, too, if he hadn't gotten cocky and patted the pocket with the letters threateningly. It turned out that that pat was one threat too far.

Angela watched as his fingers slapped against the pocket and something snapped in her mind. Why was she allowing this interloper to threaten her, and in her own house, too?

With that thought she snapped back to her normal self. The self who knew how to give orders and expected for those orders to be obeyed.

It was almost magic, how quickly she

transformed.

"Arrest him at once."

Her voice was calm, but firm. And when the officers looked at her, they wondered how there could have been any confusion. This woman had been born in charge.

One of the officer's eyes widened as he suddenly recognized Angela. He quickly whispered in his fellow officer's ear and was satisfied by the shocked expression on the man's face when he, too, realized who the woman was.

They exchanged a nod, then each of the officers grabbed one of Douglas's arms and turned him to the door. Jane took advantage of Douglas's stunned silence to reach into his pocket and snag the packet of letters.

"I'll take these."

Without another word, the policemen marched Douglas out the front door and it slammed closed behind them.

CHAPTER 32

AS THE ECHO OF the door slam faded away, so did the strength in Angela's knees. She sank into the chair and held her hands out to her daughter.

Jane handed her mother the packet of letters, but she otherwise kept her distance. There were things she needed to say to her mother. Things she couldn't say if she immediately crumpled back into little-girldom.

But Angela was too busy to notice Jane's distance. She wanted—*needed*—to make sure nothing was missing from her beloved stack of letters. Not so much as a mumble crossed her lips until she had checked the last envelope, lovingly lined all the edges up, and retied the bow. Then she gave a huge sigh of relief.

"Janey," she said as she relaxed against the back of the chair, "I'm so sorry. It's my fault—"

"Would it matter if I were a boy?" Jane interrupted abruptly. Her voice was stern and serious.

"What?" Angela sprang upright, all thoughts of relaxation fleeing at the underlying sound of pain in her child's voice.

"If I were your son, instead of your daughter," Jane explained. "Would that man have been able to threaten you? Threaten to ruin my future like that?"

"Jane, I don't think you should—"

Angela was shocked silent as Jane squeezed into the chair beside her mother. She loved her daughter and hugged her on occasion, but the two of them in a single chair?

Jane saw that her mother was surprised at the chair sharing and explained.

"Maddie told me she often sits with her mother like this, so I thought I'd try it."

"I see," Angela said. And she did see. So, she wrapped her arms around Jane and squeezed tight.

When she felt the hug had gone on long enough she shifted her weight over to one side, to give Jane more room, then twisted so she could at least partially face her daughter.

"Go ahead, daughter."

"That's just it." Jane pinned her mother with her eyes. "Do you regret having a daughter? Mommy, would you rather I was a boy?"

"Good Lord, no!" Angela blanched whiter than a cloud on a summer day at the thought. "I love you exactly as you are."

"Even though I'm weak and useless?"

"Weak and...?"

Angela twisted herself into a horribly awkward position as she tried to grab her daughter by her shoulders. But she didn't care. She'd do anything to ease the pain in her child's eyes.

"Jane! Why would you—?"

"You're fighting to keep the vote from women." Jane explained calmly. Too calmly. Angela could see there was another emotion brewing just beneath the surface, but she wasn't sure which emotion it was. "Because women need to be protected. Taken care of."

Angela opened and closed her mouth several times, but the added oxygen flow didn't help. She couldn't find the words to explain why she had sided with those who wanted to deny women the right to vote. Now that her mind had been changed, all the old arguments had turned to dust and blown away.

"Because we're *weak*!" Jane's arms burst toward the ceiling and threw Angela's arms away from her shoulders.

The burst of action felt good and she wanted more. She thought of jumping out of the chair, and maybe even running from the room. But she was wedged in the chair so tight she'd never be able to do it with any degree of dignity. So, she did the next best thing. She turned her face away from her mother.

Angela could see that Jane's breathing had become quick and shallow, a sure sign that the child was angry.

So that was the hidden emotion. She'd had no clue Jane even paid attention to the Suffrage movement. They could have talked about it together. She could have explained why it was best—

After a moment of shock—during which she realized that until recently she'd been on the wrong side of the argument—she enveloped Jane in a good, old fashioned, motherly hug.

"I'm sorry, Janey. Never, *never*, have I thought of you as weak. You're the strongest girl I know."

"Girl." Jane harrumphed. "But not as strong as a boy?"

Angela squeezed Jane even tighter, if that

was possible.

"You're the strongest *person* I know, boy or girl."

"So…" Jane wriggled out of her mother's arms and twisted around so she could see her face. "You don't think *all* women and girls are weak?"

"Of course not!" Angela grabbed Jane for another quick hug, then didn't fight it when the girl pulled away again.

A sliver of self-doubt reared its ugly head. Had she changed her position too soon? Was her first instinct, the instinct to keep women protected, the right one?

She'd never talked about serious issues with her daughter before. Maybe now was the time to start.

"Janey." Angela took a deep breath and remembered one of the recurring arguments of the red rose group. "The problem is that the right to vote can't be given only to the strong women, or the educated ones. Laws don't work that way."

Jane nodded several times as she thought that through.

"Mother?

"Yes dear."

"Remember Tom, the postman's son?"

"Certainly, I do." Angela smiled. "We gave him a job at the factory sweeping up. The poor boy is sweet as pie, but no more brains than a mosquito."

"Can he vote?"

Angela looked at her daughter. The girl had brains, no doubt about it.

"Point taken," Angela said with a grin.

The front door slammed, and a few seconds later Philip, Becca, and Maddie shoved through the doorway.

"Was that Douglas we just saw?" Philip asked.

"It looked like he was being dragged away to jail," Becca said.

"Arrested!" Maddie added, with more glee than was absolutely necessary.

"He was being..." Angela paused for a moment as she figured out what she wanted to say. "Rather threatening. Jane had him arrested."

"What about the letter?" Philip asked quickly.

Angela stiffened. How did Philip know about the letters? Did everybody in town know her business? They would have to sell the house and move—

Jane felt her mother stiffen and realized

what she was probably thinking. She put a calming hand on her arm.

"The one to Harry Burn?" Jane asked, and she gave her mother's arm a squeeze to make sure she heard.

Angela heard and relaxed. Her secret was safe.

"I'd check the police station," Jane suggested.

"That's right!" Becca turned to explain the Philip. "We had to empty our pockets when they locked us up."

"We know exactly where to look for the letter," Maddie grinned. Then her grin slipped, and her forehead crinkled, as she tilted her head to the side and added, "Well...kinda."

CHAPTER 33

ALL WAS QUIET IN NASHVILLE, especially at the police station.

The prisoner had been locked up in a cell and was currently dreaming about a bar in the twenty-first century he often visited. The paperwork had been filed, and there was a shared feeling among the night shift officers of a job well done. It was rare they got the chance to provide direct service to the upper crust of Nashville's society. It was the type of thing that ended in commendations.

Good for the career, and good for the pocketbook.

Officer Jones was less worried about a possible commendation than he was about his next nap. The added excitement caused by an arrest at one of the big houses had gotten to him. He was plumb tuckered out. Exhausted even.

It seemed to him that the patrolmen were taking longer than usual to get back to their beats. But it finally happened, the last one headed back to the streets. Before the door could click closed, Officer Jones was in his favorite chair with his feet propped up on a nearby desk.

It took exactly one minute and twenty-three seconds for Officer Jones to get in the zone, that wondrous place where stress was nonexistent, and dreams were the norm.

If left to himself Officer Jones would sleep his way to retirement. And he was left to himself a lot.

It was into this slumberous setting that Philip intruded when he opened the door of the police station and poked his head inside. He couldn't believe his good luck when he saw that Officer Jones, the only policeman visible, was sound asleep behind the counter. He signaled for Maddie and Becca to follow him inside.

But nothing is ever as easy as it could be, and Philip's first step into the station resulted in a *squeak* loud enough to wake the dead.

The dead, maybe, but not Officer Jones. He simply snorted, snuggled deeper into his chair, and then slid right back into the zone.

Surprised, yet elated, that Officer Jones had no intention of waking, Philip took a second step, only to again have the floor complain with a loud, obnoxious *squeak*.

This time the noise made Officer Jones mutter in his sleep. Not a good sign, but at least his eyes stayed closed.

Philip was calculating the likelihood of the entire floor being composed of squeaky floorboards when Maddie took matters into her own hands. She pulled off her shoes and took a step.

Silence. Blissful, wonderful, glorious silence.

Becca followed her sister's lead, and even Philip decided to remove his footwear.

But where Becca and Maddie were successful at making soundless steps on the floor, Philip was not. Without any need for words it was decided that Becca and Maddie would tiptoe across the floor to the counter where the prisoner's effects were kept.

They reached the counter without any problems and tiptoed around it to find a series of ten built-in drawers. Slowly, starting at the top, they inched the drawers open so they could search them for the letter.

All was going well until one of the drawers near the bottom stuck, and Becca and Maddie had to each grab a side and pull hard.

The resulting *screech* seemed to disturb Officer Jones. He paused his snores long enough to scratch his nose and twist his body away from the girls. But since his eyes remained closed the girls locked eyes, and slowly and carefully slid the drawer all the way open.

A smile lit up their faces as they realized they had hit the motherlode. The drawer was full of all the odds and ends that had been confiscated from various prisoners.

At that moment Philip heard a noise outside and, worried that a patrolman might have returned, he decided to check it out. But as luck would have it, even moving toward the door cause an obnoxiously loud *squeak*.

Officer Jones opened his eyes and the trio instantly froze in place. But Officer Jones was a determined man, determined to get his nap. The policeman's eyes remained focused on the stream he dreamt he was fishing in, and it was fewer than three seconds before his eyelids were down and the gentle snores had resumed.

Becca and Maddie breathed a silent sigh of relief. The glare they aimed at Philip was met with a shrug of his shoulders. How was he to know that if the floor squeaked when he was going in one direction it would also squeak when he went the other?

Becca rolled her eyes and turned her focus back to the contents of the drawer. The letter to Harry Burn had been shoved into a corner, so she grabbed the letter and showed it to her sister. Together they closed the drawer, then raced to the door, all without making a single sound.

Pausing only long enough to grab their shoes, Maddie and Becca were out the door in a flash. Philip grabbed his shoes and followed them out.

All would have been well—if Philip's jacket hadn't caught on the inside door handle and slammed the door closed. Officer Jones was startled awake and jumped up in surprise, unsure what had awakened him.

He looked around suspiciously, but his eyes refused to focus so he saw nothing unusual. They certainly didn't see the jacket stuck in the closed door. Nor did they see the door silently open and Philip's hand reach in to unhook the jacket from the knob.

But Officer Jones's ears were working perfectly, so when he heard the door click closed, he recognized the sound.

Without further ado, he stomped to the door, not caring about the cacophony of floorboard *squeaks* and *shrieks* he left in his wake. When he got to the door, he jerked it open, fully expecting to catch a juvenile prankster snickering outside.

"Gotcha!" he yelled in the gruffest voice he could manage while still half asleep.

But there was no one. No one at all.

He stuck his head through the open door and swept the street outside with a glare. If anyone was hiding outside, he wanted them to know he was on duty and in charge.

"If I catch you hooligans…" he growled, and he used the frustration he felt from being awakened from his nap to project that growl loud and far.

He got no response. No one jumped out of hiding and ran away. No one snickered from the bushes. No one gasped in fright while they cowered in the darkness.

"Must have dreamed it," Officer Jones muttered. But to be on the safe side, he growled threateningly as he sent another glare around.

Satisfied there would be no further trouble, he slammed the door closed and *squeaked* his way back to his favorite chair.

As he aimed his rump toward the chair a dog barked in the distance and he froze, mid-sit. He stayed in this position, head tilted for optimum listening, until the dog quieted again.

Then he lowered his ample bottom into the cushiony chair with a sigh. He'd had more than enough excitement for one night.

But try as he might, he couldn't rest. He'd spent years honing the instincts that had kept him safe while out on patrol. Those instincts told him he'd missed something. That something wasn't right.

His gaze swept the station, searching for any sign of change. But he found nothing. Everything was in place.

Satisfied, he decided that it hadn't been instinct, but imagination. No longer worried, he stretched his arms over his head and released the last bit of tension from his body. With the tension gone he could feel an itch in his underarm that quite simply needed his full attention. After a full minute of the most heavenly scratching possible, the itch was vanquished, and Sergeant Jones was a happy man.

As happy as he could be, anyway, when retirement was still a few months away. But he'd get there. One nap at a time.

Speaking of naps—

He melted back into his chair, put his feet on a nearby desk, and allowed his eyes to flutter closed. When another dog barked, this one quite a bit farther away, he decided to ignore it and keep his eyes closed.

Two minutes later, he was again in the zone. His own particular brand of snores blended with the ticking of the clock to create a symphony of sleep, and of the night.

CHAPTER 34

AT THE MANSION THE next morning the dining room was set for a sumptuous breakfast.

An onlooker would probably expect to find some sign of the drama that had occurred the night before. Blackmail was a dirty business. The taint of an attempt, even a failed one, usually left behind a stench of fear and loathing that was hard to get out of the carpets and drapes.

But Angela was smart. She knew that the best antidote for most kinds of nastiness was fresh air and sunshine. So, she had ordered the curtains drawn and the windows opened, and now everything was right again. For who could worry about things past while sunlight bathed the world in gold and a gentle wind played tag with the curtains?

Angela and Jane were already at the table,

each with a full plate of biscuits, bacon, and scrambled eggs, when Becca and Maddie entered wearing dresses.

"What's this?" Angela asked, her eyebrows shooting nearly to her hairline in surprise.

"They're Jane's." Becca twirled to model the dress.

"I know they're Jane's. I bought them for her." Angela smiled kindly. There wasn't an ounce of grumpiness in her heart and she wanted to make sure the girls knew it.

"She convinced us to wear them," Maddie began.

"Said the world needs to see more strong girls," Becca continued.

"And since we're strong," said Maddie.

"And we're girls," added Becca.

"It would help if we looked the part." As Maddie finished the tag team explanation, she indicated the dress she wore.

Angela's eyes twinkled as she called the girls over to inspect them. After straightening Becca's crooked bow and brushing a spot of lint from Maddie's shoulder, she nodded her approval.

"You look fine, girls." She smiled cheerily. "Now let's eat. I'm hungry."

"So am I!" Maddie grinned. "I feel like I

haven't eaten—"

But before anyone could find out how long it seemed to Maddie since she had eaten, Philip stumbled into the room. His appearance shocked them all. It was more than the bags under his eyes, which were enormous. Overnight he had grown the beginnings of a beard and had somehow sprouted a crop of porcupine quills to go along with it. And then there were the multitude of leaves and sticks and thorny vines that had attached themselves to the most unusual places.

To put it politely, he looked a mess.

"What happened—" Angela began, but she didn't get very far with her question.

"They're voting!" Philip interrupted, less worried about his personal hygiene than what they might still need to do to fix the timeline. "We've gotta go!"

"The letter?" Maddie asked.

"Has it." Philip gave a satisfied nod. "Security was tight. I was in the bushes all night. But I watched him read it this morning when I gave it to him."

Becca and Maddie nodded, relieved to hear that Philip had been successful in his mission. Becca pulled a sheet of paper and a pencil from a hidden pocket, and soon she and Maddie were drawing furiously, passing the pencil back and forth as needed.

Angela, who intended to watch the vote, stood, fully expecting the girls to follow suit. Jane did, but the other two girls remained seated.

"Girls." Angela kept her voice soft and beguiling. "We should get going."

But Becca and Maddie didn't seem to hear. They finished the drawing and began to study what they had drawn.

"Girls." Angela tried again, this time with a touch of authority in her voice. "Time to go."

Again, the girls seemed not to hear. They used their fingers to trace a line that had been drawn heavier than the rest, then locked eyes and smiled.

"Girls!" Angela commanded, tired of being ignored. "Let's go! It's voting time."

"We're hungry," Maddie said, as if it was the answer to a question. As Becca folded the paper and shoved it and the pencil back into her pocket, Maddie stubbornly crossed her arms and looked pointedly at the food.

Philip sighed as Becca and Jane crossed their arms in solidarity. As much as he trusted those charts the girls drew, he wanted to watch the vote for himself. He needed to see the

Nineteenth Amendment ratified. He needed proof that the timeline had been restored.

Unfortunately, hungry children could be very stubborn. No one was going anywhere until they had a chance to eat.

Unless—

"Do this," Philip shouted as he grabbed a biscuit and ripped it in half. He then added a bit of egg and a couple strips of bacon to the bottom section of the biscuit, and laid the top section on top, sandwich style.

When he held it in the air for all to see Angela made a face, as if it were the most disgusting thing she had ever seen.

"Annabel taught me this," Philip explained. "Said they were called muffin-macs."

Maddie opened her mouth to tell Philip what they were really called, but Becca gave a warning shake of her head. Maddie shrugged instead.

"I'm game," she said as she gathered the ingredients to make a muffin-mac for herself. Becca and Jane quickly followed suit.

Angela, reluctant to try this new way of eating, resisted until her daughter took a big bite and smiled. When she saw Jane liked the breakfast sandwich, she made one of her own.

"Not bad," she admitted after she'd taken a

bite.

"Come on." Philip grabbed a second biscuit and made a muffin-mac for the road. "We can eat on the way!"

Muffin-macs in hand, the group headed to the capitol to watch history being made.

CHAPTER 35

THE GROUNDS OF THE capitol building were crowded. And not the normal say-excuse-me-and-walk-sideways kind of crowded, either. Bodies were pressed so tightly together that a person needed to worry more about staying on her feet so she wouldn't be trampled rather than whether she'd be thought of as polite or not.

It was worse than a school of sardines, the bodies were so dense. It was a school of sardines trapped in a maelstrom, being pulled ever closer to its deadly center.

The troupe dove into this sea of bodies after only a slight hesitation, and as could be expected, they immediately became separated from one another.

Philip was the first to make it to the observation gallery. It was easy for him since he was a big, intimidating-looking guy. Those who didn't move out of his way, he shoved to the side, football-style. He made it to the rail of the balcony in two minutes flat.

Angela arrived second and had used a very different technique. She simply looked down her nose at those she wanted to move out of her way, and like magic a path was cleared.

It's not like anyone would stand in the way of the woman who controlled three-quarters of the jobs in town. She was the hot iron to the crowd's butter.

But the girls, who were neither intimidating nor in charge of companies, had to employ a third technique. They were fortunate that the three of them had locked hands early on and had been able to keep together. And when Maddie remembered how effective elbows could be when applied to the rib region, well, a plan was born.

The three girls stuck together and applied those elbows with the same precision professional loggers use to clear trees. The loud groans, ouches, and moans that followed the girls' path were a testament to their effectiveness as they chopped a path through the overgrown mass of humanity.

Jane squeezed in next to her mother as

Becca and Maddie slid in beside Philip. They were so happy to have reached their destination that they didn't notice the largish man who rammed his way to the rail beside them. Not that it mattered. As soon as he saw the size of Philip and that the girls were in the protective custody of Angela, he decided it was better to slink away to nurse his bruised ribs elsewhere.

"What's going on?" Maddie asked as she leaned over the rail to see what was happening on the legislative floor. Philip grabbed her shoulder, worried there'd be a replay of the wall climbing stunt. But when Maddie showed no signs she planned to throw her leg over the rail and climb down the wall again, Philip relaxed.

"That guy called for a vote to table." Philip pointed to a man at front of the legislative floor.

Angela, who had only arrived a few seconds before the girls, looked where Philip was pointing and nodded.

"That's the Speaker, Walker," she explained. "He's against ratification, and by far the most powerful man down there."

"What does 'vote to table' mean?" Jane wanted to know.

"If they table it, they won't even vote on it." Angela sighed, and in that sigh was a world of disgust and disappointment. "So no ratification."

Philip looked at Angela.

"You're for ratification now?"

Angela nodded.

"I realized—"

"Philip!" Becca interrupted. "Did you notice what Harry Burn voted?"

By this point Becca and her sister were both hanging over the rail, craning their necks so they could see as much as possible of the legislative floor. It was a precarious position, but Philip maintained his sanity by holding on to the big bows on the backs of their dresses.

"He voted for it to be tabled." Philip shook his head in disgust. "I thought getting the letter to him would be enough. But he's sticking with the red roses. We need a miracle—"

There was a sound from below. Philip jerked Maddie and Becca away from the rail and placed them firmly behind him.

"Wait here," he said. He took their spot so he could hang his long body over the rail. He was only upside down a few seconds, and when he pulled himself upright his face was as white as a sheet and his normally straight back was slouched in defeat.

"It's been tabled," he sighed. "It's over. There won't be a vote. We failed."

Before Philip had a chance to wallow in the heartbreak of their failure, another commotion on the legislative floor erupted. He made room at the rail so that Becca and Maddie could join him there. This time the action seemed to be happening near the front of the room.

"Who is that?" Philip was pointing to a man who had suddenly become the focus of all eyes. His jaw was set stubbornly, yet he somehow managed to look ashamed of himself.

"Banks Turner," Angela replied. "An avid anti. What's he doing?"

The tension on the legislative floor, which was intense, was focused on Turner. Those in the balcony couldn't hear what was being said, but they could certainly feel the drama.

Angela caught a couple of words from the floor and an amazed smile spread across her face.

"He voted to not table! There's a miracle for you, because he's an anti." Her forehead wrinkled in confusion and the next words were said musingly. "And Speaker Walker's friend."

More confusing sounds from the floor signaled another surprise.

"Speaker Walker called for a recount on tabling!" Jane said. "Why?"

But no one had an answer. They did the only thing they could do, hang over the rail, and watch the drama on the legislative floor unfold. The roses worn in the lapels of the legislators made the red/yellow division clearly visible.

On the main stage, more commonly known as the legislative floor, names continued to be called and votes voted. Then a very unusual thing happened. Speaker Walker handed his gavel to the man next to him—the legislative equivalent of passing the baton—and marched over to Banks Turner.

It happened to be Harry Burn's time to vote and the group in the balcony could clearly hear when he voted, "Aye." Which was disappointing to the time travel crowd, even if it wasn't surprising. Harry Burn had chosen to ignore the letter from his mother and do his part to kill the Nineteenth Amendment.

While the vote continued, Speaker Walker purposefully sat down in a chair next to Turner and draped his arm across Turner's shoulder. It should have been a friendly gesture, but it was not. Not when Walker was grasping his friend's shoulder so tight that his knuckles turned white. Leaning in close, Speaker Walker frantically whispered in Turner's ear. Whatever he said, he was adamant that his friend listen, and hear.

"Banks Turner," the clerk called.

Banks Turner, hearing his name over the hissing lecture in his ear, turned and gave Speaker Walker a hunted look. Then he stiffened his jaw, threw Walker's arm off his shoulders, and jumped to his feet.

"NAY!" Banks Turner yelled loudly.

The cheers from the balcony, mainly from the half of the onlookers who were adorned with yellow roses or sashes, were deafening. This wasn't a win, but it was a step in the right direction.

"The vote," the clerk proclaimed, "is 48-48. There will be no tabling."

Speaker Walker dropped his head to his hands in frustration. Then he pulled himself to his feet, shot a disgusted look at his friend, Banks Turner, and made his way to the Speaker's seat, stumbling all the while.

"What does this mean?" Becca wanted to know.

"Now they have to vote," Angela explained. "But first they'll have speeches and debates and everyone—"

A loud commotion on the legislative floor

cut short Angela's explanation of the normal voting process. Everyone craned over the rail, and after a few seconds Angela stood back and bit her lip.

"What is it?" Philip asked when he noticed Angela's worried expression.

"Speaker Walker is calling for the ratification vote. Now. No debates, no speeches."

"Why would he do that?" Maddie asked.

"The vote was a 48-48 tie," Angela mused as she thought through the ramifications. Then she nodded her head as she realized what the Speaker must be thinking.

"For ratification to happen," she explained, "it needs forty-nine votes for. Anything less and it fails. Speaker Walker thinks he's got the numbers. That the 48-48 tie will carry over."

"Does he?" Philip asked, worry writ clear on his face.

"Appears so." Angela shrugged. Whatever happened next, it was out of their hands. All they could do now was watch and hope.

Which was exactly what they did. As they leaned over the rail, they had no more idea of the outcome than any other person on the balcony.

Back on the legislative floor the clerk had already called several names and recorded several more votes. It was time for Harry Burn to give his vote.

"Harry Burn," the clerk called.

"Aye" was Harry Burn's quick response.

The vote continued, seemingly uneventful. Several more names were called, and votes given, before anyone realized that Harry Burn had voted for ratification, instead of against. Several of the red rose legislators cast angry eyes Harry Burn's way.

That upstart legislator had voted to ratify! He had betrayed them.

Harry Burn kept his head down as the murmuring on the legislative floor continued to build. He was in for it now, and he knew it. As soon as the vote was over the wrath of the red rose contingency would come down on him and come down hard.

That his fellow legislators would be angry enough to chase him through the building, or that he'd be forced to hide in the attics to avoid a beating, he hadn't a clue. He was not a time traveler. All this was new to him.

Harry Burn reached into his pocket and pulled out the ripped letter. As he read it for the fourth time, a gentle smile blossomed on his face. His mother was right. It was time for women to get the right to vote.

Whatever unpleasantness the red rose contingency had in store for him, it would be worth it. He was happy with his decision.

As the voting continued, many of the spectators in the balcony held their breath. It was down to the wire now. It looked like a miracle was going to happen and the ratification would pass.

On the legislative floor the clerk had gotten to the end of the vote. He only had one vote left to count.

"Banks Turner," he called.

Banks Turner gave no hesitation, whatsoever. He jumped to his feet, stood tall, and yelled, "Aye!"

The balcony erupted in cheers.

"The vote is complete. It's—"

Before the clerk could announce that ratification had passed, Speaker Walker jumped to his feet and yelled, "I change my vote from 'Nay' to 'Aye,' and move to reconsider."

This apparent change of heart was no such thing. Speaker Walker knew the rules, which stated that if he was on the winning side, he, as Speaker, could call for a recount within three days.

He had to change his vote from Nay to Aye.

It was the only shot he had at killing the Nineteenth Amendment once and for all.

History books record that Speaker Walker never called for that revote, but they don't record why. Whether it was a change of heart or some other reason, the vote stood, unchallenged.

There were time travel theorists who claimed it was because Douglas Whitfield's interfering influence had been pulled out of the equation when Philip, Becca, and Maddie took him back to the future with them. But that was only a theory.

On August 18 of 1920, Speaker Walker did what he could, then dropped down in his chair, seemingly exhausted. The pandemonium that erupted was so loud no one heard when the clerk gave the final vote count.

While the red rose legislators were disgusted with the turn of events—it was all that upstart Harry Burn's fault, he shouldn't have changed his vote—the yellow rose group were elated. The pro-ratification legislators on the floor tossed their yellow roses high in the air where they were met by yellow petals falling from the balcony.

Maddie and Becca watched as a veritable snowstorm of yellow rose petals filled the air.

The Nineteenth Amendment had been ratified. All was as it should be.

They celebrated with their super special, secret, sister handshake. As their pinkies twined together for the pinkie shake, a smile lit up both of their faces.

The mission had been a success. The timeline was healed.

Roses are beautiful flowers, but thousands of them left to rot on every surface of the legislature building and the grounds had another name. A mess. And whatever the political views of the cleaning crew, it's certain they grumbled and complained as they swept up the discarded flora and unceremoniously tossed them in a pile.

And that's how it should be. The roses were mere symbols of a movement. They had served their purpose.

Chapter 36

THE ROSSI FAMILY WAS in the front yard playing tag, and this time no one was on the sideline. Whether it was because Becca no longer had to worry about her hair being mussed—short hair was convenient that way— or some other reason, they were having so much fun that even the cool kids from Becca's class who walked by were jealous.

"Tag!"

Maddie flicked the brim of Becca's baseball cap as she ran by and sent it flying.

Becca used the sleeve of her shirt to wipe the sweat from her brow and waved at a group of her peers who were walking by for at least the tenth time. Then she turned to her sister and grinned.

"Missed me!"

"Did not!"

Becca's grin got wider as she pointed to the cap on the ground.

"You got the cap. Never touched me!"

With a laugh of sheer delight, Becca ran to the other side of the yard to tickle Audrey, who was busy gathering bright yellow dandelions into a bouquet.

After the tickle fest was completed to the satisfaction of both sisters, Becca threw herself on the ground next to her little sister and helped her with the bouquet.

"These for Mom?"

"No," Audrey answered firmly as she handed Becca the flowers, "por you. I'm making one por Maddy, too."

"That's sweet!" Becca took the bouquet of dandelions Audrey handed her and gave her darling little sister a hug in return.

Across the yard the game continued as Maddie decided not to argue the hat issue and to go after Zoe instead.

It was a good call. Zoe was ecstatic when she became it and immediately turned to chase her father around the yard yelling, "I'm it, Daddy! I'm it!"

Tony kept just out of reach of his daughter's flailing arms for several minutes. Then he slowed enough that she could catch him. He knew that a seven-year-old's patience lasted only so long, and it would spoil the fun if he stayed out of her reach long enough for her to became frustrated.

After she tagged him the real fun began. He decided to play the clown and "tripped" when he lunged for Zoe. Which, of course, meant that he had to do a roll to land on his feet. Then he "tripped" again as he ran after Maddie, doing the same roll. Before long he was tripping and rolling all over the yard. It was so funny that the whole family laughed until they nearly gave themselves stomachaches.

The whole family except for Audrey, that was. She was on a mission to create a beautiful bouquet for Maddie and couldn't be bothered with such nonsense. She continued to gather dandelions until she could barely hold the bouquet in her hand.

When she had arranged the flowers to her satisfaction, the child looked around the yard for her second sister. Maddie had just been tossed in the air by Tony and was grinning from ear to ear. Audrey held tight to the bouquet and ran over to join the rest of her family.

"Your turn, Zoe?" Tony asked as he turned to his third daughter.

Zoe grinned, nodded, and lifted her arms toward her dad. He tossed her into the air and was rewarded with squeals of laughter.

After Zoe got her glorious seconds of flight, she wrapped her arms around her father's neck and squeezed tight.

"I love you, Daddy, so much!" she said happily.

"I love you, too, Zoe-girl," Tony told his daughter as he returned her hug. He set her on her feet and looked at his watch.

"It's getting late. We should go do homework," Tony said. And he turned toward the house to lead the way inside.

"Wait!" Audrey yelled. "I want to ply like a pairy, too." She shoved the bunch of flowers into Maddie's hand before she ran over to her dad.

"Please, Daddy?" Audrey grabbed hold of one of Tony's legs and held on tight.

Tony made a face, like he was too tired, which Vanessa caught. She kneeled to Audrey's level and gently pulled the little girl to her side.

"Audrey, sweetie, don't you think Daddy

might need a break?"

Audrey looked up at her dad, her face full of so much love that Tony was immediately reenergized. He scooped up his youngest daughter and tossed her high in the air. She shrieked happily. As he caught her, she wrapped her arms around his neck and squeezed tight, just as her older sister had done.

"I love you, Daddy!"

One second later Tony found himself the center of a giant group hug as the other three daughters and his wife joined in.

The hug lasted for at least a full minute before Vanessa lowered her arms and stepped away.

"Your dad knows we love him," Vanessa declared. "Time for a snack, then homework."

The three older daughters let go of their father and raced to see who could reach the door first. Vanessa followed behind, shaking her head as she smiled.

Audrey, still in her dad's arms, suddenly looked grumpy.

"But I don't have homework," she complained.

"C'mon buttercup," Tony said as he lightly tapped his youngest daughter on the nose and swung her onto his shoulder. "Let's find you something productive to do."

Epilogue

Snow. It represents every child's hopes on Christmas morning. It hides the chores that have been left undone, covers the toys that have not been put away, and transforms the world into a magical land perfect for snowball fights and an entire village of snow people.

In other words, it creates the semblance of a perfect world, where all is calm and serene. But even perfect worlds have the voice of reason.

"History." This particular voice of reason belongs to Vanessa.

A bright white light obscures everything as a train blasts out of a tunnel, followed by the blare of a train whistle. Any semblance of calm is now gone.

"Set in stone," Vanessa's voice continues, all the world as if she's telling a story to one of her children. The train chugs purposefully on a long, straight track.

"Boring. Unchangeable."

Without warning the train whips around a sharp curve and out of sight.

"You can believe that if you want to—"

In the distance the train reappears and begins a long journey over a high bridge. The kind of bridge that turns dreams into nightmares in the squeamish and faint of heart.

"—But that's not the real story."

As the last echo of Vanessa's voice fades, the train completes its journey over the bridge and disappears into a dense forest. Only its smoke remains visible as it clears the trees and winds its way through the lonely countryside.

Far away, so far away it's more a memory than an actual sound, a train whistle blows.